Full Throttle

Full Throttle

Anthony Hampshire

Fitzhenry & Whiteside

Published in Canada by Fitzhenry & Whiteside,
195 Allstate Parkway, Markham, Ontario L3R 4T8

Published in the United States by Fitzhenry & Whiteside,
311 Washington Street, Brighton, Massachusetts 02135

www.fitzhenry.ca godwit@fitzhenry.ca

10 9 8 7 6 5 4 3 2 1

Fitzhenry & Whiteside acknowledges with thanks the Canada Council
for the Arts and the Ontario Arts Council for their support of our
publishing program. We acknowledge the financial support of
the Government of Canada through the Book Publishing Industry Development
Program (BPIDP) for our publishing activities.

Canada Council   Conseil des Arts
for the Arts   du Canada

ONTARIO ARTS COUNCIL
CONSEIL DES ARTS DE L'ONTARIO

Library and Archives Canada Cataloguing in Publication
Hampshire, Anthony, 1951-
Full throttle / Anthony Hampshire.
(Redline racing series)
ISBN 1-55041-564-6
I. Title. II. Series.
PS8565.A5663F84 2005   jC813'.6   C2005-905224-4

**U.S. Publisher Cataloging-in-Publication Data
(Library of Congress Standards)**

Hampshire, Anthony, 1951-
Full throttle / Anthony Hampshire.
[138] p. : cm. (Redline racing series)
Summary: With a volunteer crew and a rebuild car, Eddie is out
to prove that he can race alongside the best professional drivers
in the North American Formula Atlantic Series; but there are
other challenges to face, including keeping his team together.
ISBN 1-55041-564-6 (pbk.)
1. Automobile racing — Juvenile literature — Fiction. I. Title. II. Series.
[Fic] —dc22   PZ7.H34Fu   2005

Design by Wycliffe Smith Design Inc.
Cover photo courtesy of Eric Gilbert, Motorsport.com

Printed in Canada

For Maureen, Ali, and Cait.
You were right!
—*A.H.*

Acknowledgements

I am very grateful to my editor, Ann Featherstone, whose insight and thoroughness have greatly improved this story; and to Gail Winskill at Fitzhenry & Whiteside for her constant support and encouragement. I owe a special debt of gratitude to Justin Sofio, driver for the Mathiasen Motorsports/RLM Investments Formula Atlantic team in California, and to Cam Binder of Binder Racing in Calgary. Justin and Cam graciously adopted me as a crew member, patiently answered all of my technical questions about their Swift 008 race car, and even gave me an official team hat.

Chapter 1

Cutting A Deal

The microphone was stuffed right in my face as the TV guy yelled over his shoulder to his cameraman.

"Found him! Here he is! Roll tape!"

Before I could ask what was going on, the video camera's red light came on.

"Eddie Stewart interview, take one. Mark it... Bob, I'm here in the pit of Eddie Stewart, the rookie Canadian racing driver who just pulled Anaheim racer Bill Baker from a flaming wreck at Laguna Seca. So, Eddie, how does it feel to be a hero?"

"Well, actually I didn't really—"

He snapped the microphone away. "Come on, Eddie. Don't be modest! How could you possibly have survived that firestorm?"

"I guess because there was no firestorm," I replied.

"I was just watching the end of the Formula Atlantic race with my teammates when the accident happened, and—"

"Your teammates?"

"Yes—Herb MacDonald, my crew chief, Rick Grant, my engineer, and his sister Caroline."

This appeared to be even better.

"Wow! Keep it rolling… Eddie Stewart interview, take two. Mark it… Bob, I'm here in the pit of Eddie 'Fireball' Stewart, the rookie race driver who led his daredevil team right into the jaws of death as they pulled a crushed and screaming Bill Baker from a flaming wreck at Laguna Seca! Eddie and his team fearlessly charged through the field of race cars as they blasted by on all sides, and dove into a raging inferno to free Baker from a fiery grave!" he yelled.

This guy had to be from the Disaster Channel. Or Mars. I shook my head slowly.

"Look, it wasn't that way at all. Bill Baker lost control of his car and stuffed it into the bank, right in front of us. He was out cold and there was a fuel leak. We're racers ourselves, so we knew how to help. We jumped the fence, shut everything off and waited for the track marshals. That's it."

The TV guy dropped the microphone in frustration and looked at his cameraman. He drew a finger across his throat and said, "Cut it." He scowled at me in frustration.

"No dodging race cars?" he asked.

"No. Sorry," I replied.

"And no fire?"

"Lots of gas spraying around, but no fire."

"Baker wasn't screaming for help?"

"He was unconscious."

"And his brutally crushed body…?"

"He broke his foot, I think."

We were standing in the pit area at Laguna Seca, California, one of America's great racetracks, where I'd finished third in the Trans-Am race that morning—and been part of an unplanned rescue during the Formula Atlantic race that followed. All around us, tight packs of Champ Cars were blasting around the track, but all *this* guy wanted was to blow up a simple incident into some wildly sensational story. I'd followed racing all my life, and now that I was a driver, I understood that it was a serious sport that deserved decent sports coverage rather than shock reporting.

"Are you a sports reporter?" I asked him as he turned to walk away.

"You bet. We cover the action."

"Well, look around," I suggested. "There's about

twenty-five million dollars' worth of high-tech machinery on the track right now driven by some of the best drivers in the world. High-speed action. Real athletes. Fierce competition. That's a sports story. Why don't you cover that and forget trying to invent crash-and-burn stuff that never happened?"

He just shrugged and walked down the pit lane with his cameraman.

We had indeed rescued Bill Baker from a serious wreck, but as far as I was concerned, he was still in deep trouble. He'd come by my Aunt Sophie's motor home in our pit to say thanks, stayed for lunch, and talked about what he was going to do with his brand new Swift Formula Atlantic car now that he was out for the season with a broken foot. Rick, Caroline, and Sophie all saw the opportunity. If Baker couldn't drive his race car, then they figured that I should. Whether he knew it or not, Bill Baker was in the process of being talked into that by the master her-self—my wild aunt, Sophia Novello.

Sophie was a large, middle-aged lady full of energy and laughter. She was good at just about anything but truly excellent at two things: cooking and cutting a business deal. She had just sold her Vancouver restau-rant to some very sharp developers from Hong Kong for what I was sure was a small fortune. And I strongly suspected that another deal was in the works here. Sophie and our team manager Caroline Grant had quickly ended lunch and then whipped Baker away in his wheelchair into the pit lane crowds. They were taking him back to his pit for negotiations.

I didn't like his chances.

Chapter 2

Race Engineers and Leeches

The sound of the Champ Cars ripped through the air as my crew chief Herb MacDonald and my race engineer Rick Grant locked up Sophie's motor home. We jogged down to the end of the pit lane to catch what we could of the race. It was far too late to get out of the pit area to the track and watch them, but at least we could see some of the racing from behind the pit fences. We'd been doing exactly this for most of our lives, first as spectators but for the last three years as competitors.

Rick and I grew up together in Vancouver, and we had met up with Herb one summer at a junior high camp on Vancouver Island. Rick was a tall, slim, brilliant engineer who could design anything. Herb was even taller, built like a pro wrestler, and equally brilliant in his ability to build anything. The two of them were not only my best friends but also formed the heart of our little race team. Together we'd built and raced Formula Fords and now a Trans-Am Mustang. Someday, we planned to move up to a pro Formula Atlantic car, maybe even to a Champ Car.

Outside of a Formula One Grand Prix car, Champ Cars

accelerate, corner, and stop faster than anything in the world on four wheels. Handmade at about a million dollars each, a single-seat, open-wheeled Champ Car weighs in at about 1,500 pounds, packs 750 to 800 horsepower, and carries front and rear wings big enough to launch a small aircraft. For the driver, this means a ride from a standstill to 100 miles per hour in about 3 seconds, cornering forces that crush you into the cockpit at triple your weight, and top speeds in excess of 230 miles per hour. For us spectators within the pit area, however, it meant no more than a shattering noise and a momentary explosion of color as the Champ Cars rocketed past and then disappeared rapidly out of sight.

We watched the start and the first few laps from behind the fences but saw little. We were simply too close to see any battles for position or any drivers working the cars. At Herb's suggestion, we returned to Sophie's motor home and climbed up onto the roof. This was slightly better as we saw more of the main straight, but at best we still only caught glimpses of the cars.

In the end, we retired inside the motor home and watched the race on TV. Great. There we were, right in the pits at a Champ Car race, and the only way to actually see any of it was on TV. The races are about an hour and a half long, and at one-third distance, most of the cars stop for fuel and fresh tires. Thoroughly bored with the TV coverage after half an hour, we decided to walk back up to the garage area and try to watch some of the pit stops.

There was still no sign of Aunt Sophie or Caroline. On the way, we passed Bill Baker's pit again. Although nowhere near as large as Sophie's land yacht, Baker also had a motor home, and as his wheelchair was parked by the door, we assumed that he was inside with Sophie and Caroline. All of his equipment was packed up and his damaged Atlantic car sat quietly in the shade of an awning waiting to be returned to its trailer. As this might be our next race car, we stopped and stepped into Baker's pit to have another closer look. Rick motioned to the motor home.

"Think we should rescue them?"

"No," I replied. "If anyone needs rescuing it's probably Bill Baker and his crew."

"That's what I meant," Rick stated.

We walked over to the Atlantic car and knelt beside Herb, who was lying on the ground inspecting the front suspension.

"Well? Assuming Baker agrees, can we have it ready in two weeks?" I asked.

Herb stood up and brushed off his jeans.

"It's not that bad. Ten days tops, if we have the parts—and Baker said he did. It's basically a matter of bolting on new steering and suspension pieces. It would be a thrash, but we could fix this thing, do Milwaukee, and still get back in time to get the Mustang ready."

"You'd better check that main tub while you're at it, lad."

A new and heavily-accented British voice came from behind us. We turned to see a small, bearded, and deeply tanned man in his late thirties, leaning against the trailer. He had a warm smile and wore the bright yellow-and-black crew uniform of Raul DaSilva and Ascension Motorsports—our *favorite* guy's team. He walked into the pit, knelt down, and took a long look where the front suspension was attached.

"The Swift is a very strong design, but you could well have damage farther back. You'll want to be sure that there are no cracks in the carbon fiber and that everything lines up as it should. Otherwise, all your new bits won't matter. Start with the foundation first and make sure it's right."

He stood and extended his hand to Herb. This was going to be a major mistake. I should have warned the stranger, but I gave in to the temptation to watch his reaction instead.

"I'm Allan Tanner," he said, but the smile instantly turned to shock as his hand was taken and crushed.

"Herb MacDonald. A pleasure." The Man of Steel beamed.

I suspected that Herb really did take pleasure in demonstrating his vice-like grip to strangers—especially the ones who apparently knew something about race cars that he didn't. Rick and I introduced ourselves, but thought better of shaking hands when we noticed that the color was rapidly draining from Allan's face. He slid his right hand inside his jacket pocket like a wounded animal.

"You sure know your way around these cars, Mr. Tanner," I said.

"I should," he replied, walking over to the cockpit and checking the serial number plate behind the driver's seat.

"I actually might have built this very one. I'm the race engineer for Raul DaSilva and Ascension Motorsports now, but prior to that I was the Formula Atlantic Production Manager at the Swift factory just south of here. We did a run of fifty, and many of them are here today. Including this poor thing."

Ascension Motorsports—the big-dollar outfit from Brazil. And this guy was a real race engineer. Rick was on him like a leech.

"Mr. Tanner—"

"Please. Not so formal," he replied. "It's Allan."

"Right. Allan," Rick continued, "what are the chances of this car being ready for the next race in Milwaukee in two weeks? Realistically."

Allan walked slowly around the Swift, massaging some life back into his hand. He took his time, examining each corner of the car with a well trained eye.

"Realistically?" he replied. "It would be tight. To do it properly, the entire car has to be stripped right down to the basic tub, all damage found and repaired, then reassembled, re-jigged, set up, and tested. That's a lot to ask from ten days. And ten nights. Why do you ask?"

"Well, this isn't our car, but there's a possibility that we might get the chance to run it at the next race in Milwaukee. If we can repair it," Rick replied.

Allan smiled at his enthusiasm. "You know racing cars, then?"

This was an open door for Rick and Herb to impress a race engineer, and the two of them wasted no time. They spent the next fifteen minutes in a blur of conversation with Allan, telling him all they had learned from our days in Formula Ford and from building the Mustang. Then they told him what they wanted to learn about Formula Atlantic.

I leaned against a stack of tires and studied Allan as he listened, asked questions, pointed out critical areas of the car, and made suggestions. I learned that Allan Tanner had spent almost twenty years in the racing business in England and Europe and that he had worked on everything from shifter karts on up to professional Formula Atlantic. Maybe more. And he clearly knew the racing business inside out. The only thing I couldn't understand was why he worked for a guy like Raul DaSilva.

I soon had my answer.

Chapter 3

Raul DaSilva

T anner!"

A shrill, nasal blast stopped all conversation abruptly. The four of us turned to see a thin, dark man with smoldering, beady eyes standing next to Baker's trailer—his hands on his hips and his pointed chin jutting out. His face wore the same sneer that barely concealed the anger that always seemed to be simmering just below the surface. Raul DaSilva had arrived.

"So, is this what I pay you for?" Raul demanded as he strutted into the pit area like a peacock. "To hold private classes with our competitors behind my back?"

"No," Allan said quietly. "You pay me to run your race team. May I introduce—"

Raul cut him off with practiced skill. "Not interested. We will return to our pit. Now." Then he narrowed his gaze and took a hard look at me.

"Wait! I know you. During my victory interview yesterday, you questioned my driving, " he stated.

I met his gaze. "Yes, I did. Along with a few other people—like the chief race steward."

Raul's anger inched closer to the surface.

"No doubt you were one of the so-called 'witnesses' the steward told me had complained. Yes…and I think I see why."

Raul strutted slowly and confidently around the damaged car, hands clasped behind his back, as if he were a lawyer arguing a case in court. He stopped and looked directly at me.

"Yes, I see it now. This is the car that was damaged after ramming me in the race. You and your friends are the crew, no? And now that you have failed to discredit me, you do not know what to do. So, you come whining to my race engineer."

"Look, Raul, they're just some lads looking for some advice," Allan began, but Raul raised his hand.

"No, Tanner. That is where you are quite wrong. They are thieves. Simple thieves. They look to take from me what they do not own."

Raul spread his arms wide in a classic victim's pose.

"I employ you, Tanner. Do you forget this? If they profit from your advice then I do not. All of your knowledge, all of your experience, and all of your ideas belong to me.

I am the one who pays your six-figure salary. "

Six-figure salary? A hundred thousand bucks or more a year? I began to understand why Allan put up with this guy.

Raul continued. "So, you belong to me, Tanner. No one else. Come, there is work for you to complete," he said, snapping his fingers and turning quickly to leave. It was exactly the gesture you would use with a dog.

"And I thought slavery was dead," said Herb. "Come on, guys, let's go."

We started to walk out of Baker's pit, but something in Allan's voice stopped us.

"You didn't let me finish, Raul," Allan said slowly and carefully. He spoke in the same low tone, but now his voice had a hard edge that hadn't been there before.

"I was about to say that these are three lads looking for some basic advice. Very much like I did twenty years ago. They're not the crew for this car, as you have incorrectly assumed, but they might be given a chance to repair and race it at Milwaukee in two weeks. That's all. So they're not thieves, as you suspect. And Raul, I want you to be very clear, crystal clear actually, about something else. I do not 'belong' to you."

Raul threw up his hands in mock apology.

"Oh! Please, Mr. Tanner, will you forgive me? How could I have been so—what is the word—so insensitive?"

"Easy," Rick snapped. "You're a jerk."

That did it. Raul's anger erupted as he took two steps toward Rick and swung, hard, with his right fist. It would have connected squarely with Rick's glasses, but Herb stepped in neatly and caught Raul's fist in midflight like he was snagging a hard drive to second base. Herb tightened his grip on Raul's fist as he froze and looked up at him like a trapped rodent.

Towering over Raul, Herb leaned forward and whispered, "If you promise to act like a grown-up, I'll let you go."

Raul scowled, nodded, and was released. Then it was Rick's turn.

"Listen, Raul, I'm sorry for calling you a jerk, OK? Not real mature on my part."

Raul remained in the victim's role. "You are sorry? Good for you. So, what am I to do? Should I also now apologize?" he asked sarcastically.

"That would be the gentlemanly thing to do," Allan replied.

"I am not in the habit of apologizing," Raul said bluntly.

Allan sighed and took a few quiet moments to collect his thoughts. I had the feeling that we were about to hear something that had been building up between these two for a long time.

"Well, then there is the other alternative," Allan began. "And I suppose that this is as good a time as any. I must agree—you aren't the type to apologize, Raul. I have also learned in the past few months that you aren't the type to listen, to understand, to take advice, or to learn from a mistake. You have the best equipment money can buy, and some talent. But it won't be enough."

"You forget that I lead the championship, Tanner!" Raul stated hotly.

Allan nodded. "Yes, you do. For now. Three races remain, and you may do well in them. Perhaps even win the championship. But it will get you nowhere without the most important element for success. Respect. You have none for your cars, for your competitors, for the sport, or for people. And that is why there is now something else you don't have. A race engineer. I quit."

Raul went ballistic.

"Quit? Never! You have no right! You have signed a contract!" he screamed. When Raul was really angry all the veins popped out on his neck and on his temples, which made him look even more like a deranged weasel.

"Actually, as you're late paying me again this month, Raul, you would very likely be the one found to be in breach of contract," Allan replied. "Now would be a good time for you to leave. I'll be around shortly to collect my things. We're finished."

You are the one who is finished, Tanner! No one in racing will hire you after this! I will see to it!" Raul yelled as he stormed out of the pit.

Allan turned to us, smiled, and shrugged his shoulders. He had the air of a man who had just been released from a cold, dark place.

"Sorry you got caught up in that. It's been coming on for a while, and this was just the last straw. It's time for me to move on."

Herb slapped him on the back.

"Good move, I'd say. Come on, I'll give you a hand with your gear."

They walked off together, Allan laughing and shaking his head. Rick watched them go silently, then quickly removed his glasses and began polishing them rapidly. This was code. I knew from way back in junior high that when Rick started polishing his glasses, he had mentally entered a strange and often dangerous place. Turbo brain mode. But this time I was right with him. We both knew that an engineer like Allan Tanner was worth his weight in gold to any race team, and as of that moment he was available. We had plans for him.

Chapter 4

Assembling the Team

The door to Bill Baker's motor home burst open. Aunt Sophie, laughing loudly and waving to us, stepped out with Caroline. Sophie had some papers in one hand and she was using a tissue in the other to dab tears from her eyes. Caroline looked mildly confused, as if some hilarious scene had just been played out that had gone right over her head.

"Oh, this is always such fun!" Sophie announced as she ushered Caroline, Rick, and me out of Baker's pit and back toward her motor home.

"What's such fun? What just happened in there?" I asked Caroline.

She shrugged her shoulders. "Hard to say, exactly. It all went by so quickly. One minute they were trading stories about business, and the next minute Sophie has them all signing and passing around papers. Then they had a few more laughs and we left."

Sophie had cooked up a deal. I knew it. But a deal for what, how long, and how much were details that she would reveal to us in her own way, and in her own time. It wouldn't have surprised me if she'd whipped out the cell phone, bought back her old restaurant from the Hong Kong bankers, resold it to Baker, and flipped our Mustang, her motor home, and Rick's laptops into the deal as well. Anything was possible. The four of us walked briskly back to her motor home in expectant silence, broken only by Sophie's humming.

We arrived a few minutes later, and she sat us down at the dining table, took out five crystal glasses, and filled them with peach juice. Rick reached for his right away but had his wrist slapped smartly.

"Hands off! Where is Herbie?" Sophie demanded.

"He's helping a guy move some tools and stuff," Rick grumbled as he nursed his wrist.

Sophie frowned. "Well then, Rickie, you will please go and find him. Take Eddie. Caroline and I will wait here. Quickly now. We need to have a meeting."

"Couldn't I have my juice first?" Rick asked.

Sophie shook her head and folded her arms with determination.

"Not until we are all here. We will talk. And then we will drink. Together."

You do not argue with Sophia Novello when her mind is made up. Rick and I left again and headed back toward the Ascension Motorsports transporter. I didn't feel like another run-in with Raul, but I knew that's where we would find Herb and Allan. Rick was still moaning about the peach juice so I stopped and bought him a soda at a concession on the way. He slammed back the whole can in one go, and was about to belch out the chorus to "Burnin' Love" until I stopped him cold with a menacing glare.

The Champ Car race wailed on around us, but as ever we were stuck inside a maze of huge transporters, tow vehicles, and motor homes, so we had no idea who was winning. We were almost at DaSilva's pit when we saw Herb and Allan approaching us. Herb had two notebook computer bags over his shoulders and was pushing a huge tool cabinet. Allan, who had changed out of his uniform, was carrying stacks of binders, a duffel bag, and a large-wheeled trunk.

Rick fell into step beside Allan, and I helped push the tool chest. Herb walked beside me, grinning like he'd just won the state lottery.

"Eddie!" he whispered. "Think we've got room for these babies in the trailer?" he asked, nodding at the boxes of CDs on top of the tool chest.

I picked up one of the five blue disk boxes, opened it, and scanned the labels. They were all embossed with gold letters that read Tanner Race Engineering, and each one had neatly handwritten labels with names like Long Beach, Laguna, Milwaukee, Toronto, Miami, and Phoenix. A light went on in my head. These disks held Allan Tanner's technical data and race setup specifications for every track that the North American Formula Atlantic series visited in the course of a season. They would include detailed information that a team could use to fine-tune a Swift race car for maximum performance at every track, in any weather. These CDs were gold to any Atlantic race team.

I glanced up at Herb and returned his grin. If we were going to run Baker's car at Milwaukee in two weeks, we would at best be guessing at the proper car setup. But the information on these disks could be the difference between running at the back and running up near the front. The only catch was how to convince Allan Tanner to share it with us.

"Wow!" I whispered to Herb, carefully placing the box back on the tool chest.

"Yeah, it's the real deal," Herb stated. "And so is Allan. I found that out when we went back to

DaSilva's transporter and packed up."

"I'll bet that was special," I replied, imagining another explosion from Raul DaSilva.

Herb shook his head smiled.

"It was pretty sad, really. We're there for maybe thirty seconds when Raul comes in—only now he's all whiny, saying how sorry he is, pleading for Allan to stay, even offering him a raise. He's like, 'Allan, don't leave. I'll give you a raise.' But Allan doesn't bite—he just finishes packing up his stuff, says goodbye to all the other slaves, wishes Raul good luck, and walks out. The guy's got class, Eddie. I invited him back for dinner at Sophie's."

We arrived back at our pit, locked all of Allan's gear inside our trailer, and rejoined Sophie and Caroline inside the motor home. They were waiting patiently at the dining table, watching over the crystal juice glasses. We introduced Allan, Sophie poured a sixth glass for him, and we all squeezed around the small dining table. This was only really possible after Sophie decided to stand and then directed Herb to sit on the floor. She cleared her throat, waited for our attention, and held up a new file folder.

"Now that we are all here together, I wish to speak. First, welcome, Mr. Tanner. You will be joining us for dinner? Good. Second, I am pleased to tell you that

Mr. Baker's car is no longer for sale. We've reached an agreement to lease Mr. Baker's car for the next race. If you boys can fix it, you can race it at Milwaukee," she said, beaming.

"Yes!" Rick roared, jumping up from his seat, clanging his head on the hanging lamp, and punching his fist straight through the ceiling tile above him. The tile split into fragments, which rained down onto the table. One of smaller ones landed with a plop in my glass. I slid it over to Rick.

"This one's yours, Brainiac."

Caroline sighed as she brushed ceiling tile fragments from her shoulder and removed Rick's glasses from her hair.

"First, we'll have to fix the ceiling," she observed. "And then our Richard. If that's possible."

Rick grimaced in pain and slowly retrieved his fist from inside the ceiling.

Sophie rolled her eyes, then carried on. "Mr. Baker has agreed to transport the car back to his shop in Anaheim, where you can do the repairs."

Never one to mince words, Sophie immediately turned her attention to Allan Tanner, who was sitting quietly beside Caroline. She looked at his strong, calloused hands and deep tan, and made the connection quickly.

"Mr. Tanner, my boys have a lot of work ahead of them. They will need expert help, and I think that you're a man experienced in such things. What are your plans?"

Allan shrugged and replied, "Well, other than accepting your invitation for dinner, I don't really have any. At the moment I am, shall we say, at leisure."

"You've lost your job, then?" Caroline asked.

"Quit, actually. Up until an hour ago I was race engineer for Ascension Motorsports," Allan replied. "But as of this moment, I am—"

Sophie held up her hand and cut him off.

"A racing car engineer? Yes. I thought so. You are welcome to join us for dinner, Mr. Tanner—and also as an engineer for our team. We can offer you excellent food, luxury accommodations, and travel to Milwaukee, Wisconsin. We will also pay you three times the amount that Rickie, Herbie, and Caroline are earning."

Allan raised an eyebrow. "And exactly how much might that be, then?"

"Three times this," Caroline replied with a grin, making a zero sign with her thumb and forefinger. "But then," she continued, "there are really great side benefits. A free ride from California all the way back east to Wisconsin in this fabulous motor home. A chance to really see America. Sophie's incredible cooking. Rick's unique Elvis impersonations. Herb's special mechanical friends. I'll teach you photography. And you'll have the chance to coach one of the best new racing drivers in North America."

Allan looked over at me and raised an eyebrow. "Is that so?" he asked.

I felt the color rising in my face, to the unfailing delight of Caroline and Sophie.

"Look, Allan, with all due respect to Caroline, we're pretty new to this. I mean, I think there's a lot of raw talent sitting around this table right now, but compared to the setup DaSilva has—"

"Put that aside for a moment," Allan replied. "Just tell me why all of you want to race this car in two weeks. Why do it at all?"

No one said anything for several long moments. It was a good question—actually, the only question. And I also knew very well that it was a test.

Allan Tanner had been in the game for twenty years. He'd built and engineered top-level cars that had won all over Europe. He'd seen his share of dreamers and guys who talked big and liked the hero race driver image, but really didn't have the fire, talent, or the discipline to harness it. And he'd just left someone who would do anything to win. At any cost. Allan Tanner didn't need—and, I suspected, didn't want—any more of the same, even for one race.

Finally Herb spoke up. "We want to race because we think that we can be good at it. Someday, maybe really good. This is a chance for us to take a step up. It might just be for one race, but we're serious. We want to learn how to be professionals. It's about that simple."

"That's right," I added. "Rick understands the physics and engineering. He just sees it in his head. Always has. Herb can build or make anything you want, and he does it right the first time. Caroline could run a small country, and she knows how to organize us into a team. My aunt Sophie has known us all since we were kids, so she understands what we like, what we want, and most of all what we need. As for me, all I've ever really wanted to do is wheel a race car. And we'll do it, too. But you know what? We'll do it better with you."

Allan looked for a long moment at each of us in turn and began to smile. Then he settled back in his seat, took a sip of juice, and turned to Sophie.

"Done," he stated firmly.

And with that we had ourselves a professional race engineer.

Chapter 5

Allan's Lot

The next week was a blur of activity. It was quickly agreed by all that if there was any driving to be done, as one of the best young racing drivers in North America, I was the guy for the job. So I was dispatched, in our trusty Dodge crew cab truck and race trailer, two days north to Herb's shop in Seattle, Washington, to pick up shop equipment and supplies. Then I got to turn the rig around and drive all the way back again to Baker's shop in southern California. Altogether I spent five days watching the pavement roll by and listening to Herb's truly awful collection of CDs, most of which were commercial jingles and television show themes from the seventies.

To break the boredom I called Caroline on the cell phone each morning. I learned that everyone had quickly moved in to Bill Baker's shop and begun the task of rebuilding the damaged Swift. Herb had completely stripped it bare in a day. Allan decided what could be salvaged and what needed to be replaced, then he faxed a list of the new parts they needed directly to the factory and had them delivered overnight to Anaheim.

Rick had been going through Allan's data disks on his laptop like a kid on Christmas morning, copying files, merging databases, and rewriting his own software. For Rick, the best part was the chance to work on a real open-wheeled formula car with wings rather than the Mustang, which was, in Allan's opinion, little more than a crude "Yank Tank."

There were several different racing series for Formula Atlantic, and none of them let you change much on the car. Everyone had to run the same Swift race car with the same Cosworth engine, and they had to use the standard factory wings set to exactly the same angles. This also applied to the North American Formula Atlantic Championship. But the rules around aerodynamics and suspensions were less rigid, and teams were allowed some freedom to experiment, especially with the designs of front and rear wings.

Holding all of this activity together was Aunt Sophie, who had turned her motor home into a mini hotel, constantly supplying "real" coffee (Earl Grey tea for Allan), fresh fruit, lasagna, huge sandwiches, cookies, and—especially for Herb—pancakes to order. Allan remarked that he had seldom eaten better, which immediately endeared him to Sophie for life. Caroline was spending her time on the phone with suppliers, ordering a set of new crew uniforms, organizing the trip east to Milwaukee, and sketching designs for a new paint scheme for the Swift. We might only ever make this one Atlantic race, but we weren't going to show up looking like a bunch of greasy, wide-eyed garage rats. With an expertly rebuilt car, a race engineer, and a flashy new paint scheme and uniforms, we were going to roll into Milwaukee looking as professional as anyone.

I finally pulled into Anaheim at sunset five days later, expecting to find a beehive of activity. Instead the shop was still and quiet. Pieces of the Swift were scattered across the floor and on workbenches and tables. Allan was at a bench carefully assembling new steering parts. I saw Herb behind a glass door in a back room, building a gearbox and talking to himself—and no doubt to the gears.

"Ah, young Edward returns!" Allan announced, looking up. "Splendid trip?."

"Fabulous," I replied flatly. "A five-day feast of hot

pavement, gas stations, and dirtburgers."

"Nothing like the west coast in summer, I'm told," Allan said, smiling.

"So, where is everyone?" I asked, glancing around.

Allan tore off a paper towel and cleaned his hands.

"Rick is off at an aircraft company researching designs for some new wing ideas he's been working on. Sophie and Caroline are asleep in the motor home. We've all had some late nights. Actually, I just got up from a nap myself. I'm not sure about Herb, though. I think he's been at it nonstop for the last three days. Does he ever sleep?"

"Herb will sleep when he's ready. Actually it's more like a coma than sleep," I replied. "But not if there's a car to build. Then he'll go flat out until it's done. What about you, Allan? Still love pulling these all-nighters?"

The bare chassis tub of the Swift was sitting three feet off the floor on steel work stands. Allan walked over to the cockpit, removed the small steering wheel, and motioned for me to approach.

"Come on. Slide in. See how it fits."

I stepped onto a chair and stepped in carefully. Placing my hands on either side of the cockpit, I slowly lowered myself in and down until I was snugly reclined with my feet somewhere in front of me and a small electronic data screen at arm's length. Sitting in a Formula Atlantic car is a lot like lying in a narrow bathtub with only a small opening for your head and arms. You almost wear it. This one had a seat designed for Bill Baker, who was a bit wider and taller than me. But otherwise it felt right.

"Looks good on you," Allan said, pouring a cup of strong tea from a Thermos. "Tea? It's Earl Grey."

"No thanks. I'll need some padding around the hips, shoulders, and behind my neck, but otherwise it feels OK. So, are you avoiding my question? The all-nighters?"

Allan stirred some milk and sugar into his tea and sipped it carefully. Then he stared out the shop door for what must have been a full minute. Either the guy was a thinker or I'd said something wrong. Or maybe the tea was off. Turned out he was a thinker.

"I'm not avoiding the question. You just made me stop and reflect for a moment or two. I haven't had much time to do that lately with Raul and his gang. No, I don't much enjoy working through the night. Not anymore. Used to, though, as a young lad years ago. Started out back in London apprenticed to a Rolls-Royce agent. The Roller is a beautifully engi-neered car—especially the new ones—but there's no real spice, no danger in them. So on weekends I used to take my old BSA motorbike out to spectate at the racing circuits. I was at Brands Hatch one rainy Sunday, walking through the pits when I stopped to watch a crew trying to start a Formula Three car.

"They were going mad—shouting, swearing, throwing wrenches. It seemed obvious to me that there was no spark to the engine and so I offered a suggestion. The driver shot back that if I thought I was so clever, I should jump in and fix it myself. So I did."

"You got it going?"

"I did. It was dead simple, really—fouled plugs and wet leads. But when you're frantic you don't think straight. Anyway, I replaced the wet parts with dry ones, fired it up, and off they went. They invited me back. That's where it began. I helped out a few more weekends and they soon offered me a full-time job. I spent the next ten years traveling all over England and Europe as a racing mechanic in Formula Three and later Formula 3000. Then after that a few years in F1—"

"Formula One? Really?"

I was stunned. I knew Allan had serious race team experience, but the Formula One World Championship was the big time, "the show," the top of the ladder in international racing.

"Yes, F1. Not with any of the big three teams, mind you—although I had some offers. I was a mechanic for Osella in Italy and ATS in Germany, then race engineer with Leyton House in England and with Arrows, before they retired. Learned a lot and saw a good deal of the world."

"So why did you stop?" I asked.

Allan took another long sip of his tea, put it down, and began to fit the steering assembly onto the front of the car.

"I met Emily. She was a journalist for some glossy American lifestyle magazine doing a story on F1—the danger, the excitement, the glamour, and the human drama of international motor racing. All that sort of thing. She followed our team around for a summer. We spent a lot of time together and fell for each other in rather a big way. Things developed from there. We were both tired of airplanes, hotels, and living out of suitcases. Can't travel to eighteen Grand Prix races on five continents for nine months a year and expect to have any sort of a real life. We were both looking for something better, more permanent. And we found it in each other. It seemed like a good time to stop, to settle down, even think about a family. So I bought an expensive Saville Row suit and an engagement ring, popped the question to her right in the boarding lounge at Heathrow Airport, and we were engaged. Emily was a California girl and wanted us to live near the ocean. And Swift Engineering out here was look-ing for someone to oversee production of their new Atlantic car. It all fit nicely. So I left England, took the job with Swift, put a down payment on a small house…."

Allan's voice trailed away. He placed the eight mounting bolts for the steering assembly and then began to carefully tighten each one in turn to the exact torque. He finished his tea and set the cup down slowly. Clearly, this was difficult ground for him, and he needed some time. Silently I replaced the removable steering wheel.

"She'd told the magazine that she was leaving. She'd just finish up one final story for them on the new oilfields in northern Russia, then go back home to her Mum's for Christmas. Russian airlines went on strike—they do that over there quite regularly, especially during the holidays. So she hired a small private plane to make a connection back to Moscow and then on to New York. Anxious to get back to California, you see—decorate the tree, roast turkey, plum pudding. Start new…"

"And something happened," I said.

"Her plane went down in a blizzard somewhere in the Ural mountains. They looked for a while. I even went back myself and flew over the same flight path for a week. No one ever found it. "

I stared at the small steering wheel in my hands for a long time and began to understand that there were many layers to Allan Tanner. And here I was, wondering why he was building me a race car in a small shop in California instead of sitting on the beach with his wife and playing with their kids.

"How long?" I asked.

"Two years ago last Christmas," Allan replied. "I thought it best to leave California, and I had a few contacts in the States. Actually, this is the one country I'd never seen much of. One call led to another, and I signed on with Raul DaSilva in Florida to do the North American Atlantic series. Not one of my better decisions."

He walked back to a workbench, replaced his tools, and then turned to me with a slight smile and said, "And now here I am with you lot. Funny how things work out sometimes, isn't it?"

"Nothing funny about it," said a deep voice from the back of the shop.

We glanced over to see Herb, who had come out of the engine room and had obviously been listening for a while.

"Know what I think? You're supposed to be here with us, Allan. If we're ever going to put this car back together and do anything with it, we need you. And in a different way maybe you need us, too. You're not here by accident. That's how I see it anyway."

"Perhaps you're right," Allan replied after a pause.

Then it was all business. "Right then. Come on, Edward. Out of the car. We've got a lot of work to do."

Chapter 6

Waiting

We were down to four days. Bill Baker stopped by with some more papers for Sophie, wished us well, and promptly limped off with his family to Hawaii. Allan, Herb, and Rick basically locked themselves inside the shop and spent every waking hour putting the Swift back together. Sophie ran the motor home hotel and restaurant day and night.

I knew Caroline was a talented artist and ace photographer, but she also proved to be a natural team manager. She took on ordering supplies, licensing, contacting the race organizers in Milwaukee, handling the entry, motel reservations and insurance, and planning our route. She even designed and launched our own website, for our legions of fans around the world to use—with a full photo gallery, team profiles, news updates, and an e-mail link. So far only our parents had e-mailed us, but I still thought it was very cool to have a slick website. We just needed a race car to go with it.

Again I was the go-fer, as in, *Hey, Eddie, go-fer groceries, go-fer parts, to the dry cleaners, to the airport*…and so on. Although this was my usual role before a race, it never seemed to let up. As soon as I returned from one errand, someone had a new one for me and off I went again. Often in the middle of a trip, I'd get a call on the cell phone to pick up this or that on my way back. I was rarely in the shop. I began to wonder if somehow they really didn't want me working on the car, or getting involved with the preparations.

After returning to the motor home from my fourth delivery run of the day, it started to get to me. Caroline had just got off the phone with a paint shop across town.

"Excellent! All the bodywork is painted and ready to go. When can you pick it up, Eddie?"

I stopped in the middle of putting lettuce in the fridge.

"Who knows?" I snapped. "I mean, I've got to put the vegetables away first, Caroline. Lettuce was on sale today, so I made an executive decision and bought four, count 'em, four bunches. And no, I didn't forget to get your favorite animal cookies either. And now, I'll probably need to go do the laundry again, or maybe Allan has more parts coming in from England, so I guess I really don't know if I'll have time to pick up the bodywork as well. It's hard to say."

Caroline got up from the dining table, which had become her office and design studio. Then she stretched the kinks out of her back and came over to find her package of cookies. She opened them and passed me one.

"Here. Have a giraffe."

I took it and bit the head off.

"It's the waiting, isn't it?" she asked.

I nodded, finished off the giraffe, and reached for a sea lion.

"It's like that circus family of high-wire walkers— the Flying Wallendas," I told her. "Somebody asked them once what it felt like being up there, a hundred feet off the ground, balanced on a thin strand of wire with no safety net. They just said that the wire was life. Everything else before and after was just waiting."

Caroline considered this as she pushed her long blonde hair back behind her ear.

"So, then this isn't real life?"

"No. It's real enough," I replied. "But it just feels like I'm standing in a line that never moves. I need to get to Milwaukee. I need to get in that car."

"You need to get out on the wire," she added.

Caroline gave me one more cookie—an elephant this time—took one for herself, and put the package in the cupboard. She crossed to her desk, picked up a piece of paper with an address on it, and handed it to me.

"If you leave now, you can get there before they close. And on the way, maybe you could spare a thought for the five of us. We're all working like mad fools to get this car ready for one race 2,000 miles away next week. One shot at full throttle on that oval, and that's it. All or nothing. And none of us are doing it just for fun, Eddie. We're doing it for you."

"Because I'm such a hotshot race driver, right?"

"I don't know. Maybe. I know that the guys think so. We'll see soon enough. As for me, it's the creative and artistic challenge of seeing all of those pieces come together into something powerful. And also because you're just so fabulously cute," she chirped over her shoulder as she left the motor home, slamming the door behind her.

An hour later, as I sat stuck in rush hour traffic on the west side of Anaheim, I decided it was time to quit being a whiner. I had been looking at this whole deal purely through my own eyes, only really focusing on what I wanted. I was part of a team, not in charge of a group of slaves. I imagined myself for a moment as Eddie DaSilva, screaming till the veins popped out on my forehead. I didn't want to become that. They were all working hard at what they did well, and it was my job to be patient and support them while they did it. If everything went according to schedule, in a week's time it would be my turn to bring all their hard work together on the one-mile oval in Milwaukee. Caroline was right. And—I smiled to myself—pretty fabulously cute herself.

I finally arrived at the paint shop five minutes before closing and backed the truck up to load the body panels. The Swift's bodywork was made up of a bullet-shaped nose cone, a front wing, two side pods that covered the radiators, a long top section from the nose back to behind the roll bar, an engine cover, and end plates for the rear wing. All of it was handmade from lightweight carbon fiber and attached to the car with flush aircraft fasteners. Baker had provided us with two full sets of bodywork and wings, plus two spare nose cones, and Caroline had sent all of it over with detailed drawings and instructions.

As I got out of the truck, the shop owner met me and asked me to follow him back to his office. Caroline's designs for the Swift's bodywork were top secret, known only to herself and Sophie, so I was anxious to see what the finished product looked like. I had also learned that it was smart business to carefully inspect the job before settling the bill. I was ready to do both before handing over my credit card. But I discovered that other plans had been made.

I was given an envelope which contained a three-page bill for $3,897.50. My jaw was on its way to hitting the floor in shock when I noticed a small note attached to it with a phone number. The note instructed me to call the number before paying. I grabbed the cell and dialed. I got a familiar answer after the first ring.

"Eddie. This is you?"

Aunt Sophie.

"Yes, Sophie, of course it's you—I mean me. Guess where I am."

"I know this," she replied confidently. "You are at the paint shop. You are holding the bill. And you sound upset. I am pleased."

"Well, you won't be pleased when you see this bill. It's almost four grand! Who is paying for this?"

I heard a whispered side conversation and some

muffled laughter on the other end, and then Sophie cleared her throat and took a very businesslike tone.

"That amount does not surprise me, Eddie. It is fair. It was a rush job and quite complicated. No matter. Pay it and come home."

"Not until I've been over every inch of that body-work."

"You can't. I left instructions for it to be wrapped."

"Wrapped?"

"Yes, Eddie, it is wrapped like… Never mind. Just keep it that way and don't touch it. Drive carefully," she ordered and hung up.

I paid the manager and went back the shop to find fourteen pieces of bodywork in the back of the truck, each wrapped snugly in white paper and tied down.

I drove slowly back to Baker's workshop with one eye on the road and the other on the rearview mirror, ensuring that all the pieces stayed secure. Caroline and Allan were waiting for me when I arrived, and without a word, the two of them immediately unloaded the packages and whisked them into the shop. My offers of assistance were politely but firmly refused, and Sophie marched me into the motor home and sat me down with Herb and Rick to a full Italian dinner. Clearly the three of us had been banished from the shop and were being held prisoner by the

irresistible force of Sophie's cooking.

Between mouthfuls, I was delighted to learn from Rick that the Swift had been fully repaired and assembled. Herb confirmed that a fresh engine had arrived, the gearbox was assembled, and both were installed. All that remained was to fit the bodywork and pack up for the four-day trip to Milwaukee. I couldn't wait. I gulped down the last of my cannelloni, wiped my mouth, and sprang up from the table. I felt a firm hand on my shoulder pushing me back down into my seat.

"Not yet," Sophie commanded. "You three wait here until I return. Have dessert," she added, passing around the box of animal cookies.

We sat in silence for a few moments trying to figure out what was up. We were sick of cookies. Sick of waiting. The moments stretched into half an hour. Rick and I were both pacing the narrow confines of the motor home and running into each other while Herb surfed through the dozens of channels on the TV, finally settling on a Hindi musical about pirates on the Ganges River. After a while we all started to watch it. Herb was even humming along to some of the choruses.

Too many late nights will do strange things to you. Finally, Sophie returned with a grin on her face like

Full Throttle

the Cheshire cat. "Come," she said simply and led the way into Baker's shop.

The Swift was down on its wheels again, but completely covered with a large canvas tarp. Standing together behind the rear wing were Allan and Caroline, beaming in new crew uniforms. They were wearing short-sleeved, button-down shirts of crisp white oxford cloth with their first names embroidered in gold on the pockets, and tailored, black pants with razor-sharp creases. Then, with a nod from Caroline, Allan snapped back a tarp to reveal the transformed Swift.

Caroline had designed a paint scheme in a rich shade of metallic candy-apple red, which began at the nose and gradually blended into a deep crimson as it flowed back the length of the car to the engine cover. There were no numbers or sponsor names anywhere—just "Eddie" neatly scripted in small gold letters on either side of the cockpit. The whole car shimmered like deep water at sunset. Just sitting there, it looked clean, cool, and bullet-fast. Best of all, it had my name on it.

"There's more," said Caroline.

There was more. She opened a huge cardboard box and produced identical crew uniforms for everyone else and a second box containing two red driving suits, gloves, shoes and a new helmet painted in the same liquid shades of red. Herb and Rick immediately tore into the boxes and raced each other into the tiny washroom to try on their uniforms. I just knelt beside the Swift, watching the light play over the rich, deep layers of paint and ran my hand slowly over the cool, smooth surfaces. I looked up at Caroline.

"It's beautiful, Caroline."

She smiled with satisfaction.

"I know. It's art."

Allan sat on one of the rear tires and checked his watch.

"It's as pretty a racing car as I've seen in a long while. Nothing like a fast red car, I always say. And these uniforms are rather smart. But let's not just hang about ogling everything, shall we?"

He stood, flicked a piece of lint from his new shirt, and looked up.

"Ladies and gentlemen…let's go motor racing."

Chapter 7

Bad Hair Day

After the unveiling of the rebuilt Swift, we spent the rest of the weekend packing up and preparing our truck, trailer, and motor home for the long haul east to the next Atlantic race in Milwaukee, Wisconsin. Covering over 2,000 miles and seven states—crossing the country from the Pacific Coast to the shores of Lake Michigan—was no small trip. We packed everything we could think of into the vehicles and left Anaheim at sunrise on Monday. Driving 500 miles each day would bring us into Milwaukee on the following Thursday evening. The first practice session on the one-mile oval was set for Friday morning.

Herb and I took the Dodge tow truck and the race car trailer. Rick, Allan, Sophie, and Caroline followed in the motor home. Our first day took us east on

Interstate 40 through the blistering heat of the Mojave Desert, over the mountains, and into Albuquerque, New Mexico. Herb insisted on taking the first shift behind the wheel of the tow truck. He lasted all of fifteen minutes, then informed me that he felt a little tired. I took over and he stretched out across the back seat "for a short snooze." I drove the truck the rest of that day and all of the next three.

All of us had spent years traveling in the States or Canada and were used to the long hours of highway travel on shimmering blacktop. Not Allan. His road trips were limited to England and Europe, where you can get almost anywhere in a day, and even cross several different countries in a weekend. Driving for four days straight and not even leaving the country was a major adjustment. Rick told me that Allan had fallen asleep near Albuquerque and woke up hours later in Clinton, Oklahoma. Looking out the window at exactly the same landscape, he demanded to know why we had stopped for five hours. Rick gave him a map and a lecture on the size of the United States.

When we did stop, it was only to assemble in the motor home for a meal or to overnight in an RV park. Sophie and Caroline took the rear bedroom. Herb preferred to spend his nights sleeping in the trailer to keep the Swift company—and maybe tell it a bedtime story or two. Allan, Rick, and I took the foldout bunks in the front of the motor home, which were quite comfortable, aside from Rick's incessant snoring. Traffic was usually light, and the flat, sun-bleached landscape rolled by at a leisurely pace. We cruised through Albuquerque to Amarillo, Texas, and then on to Oklahoma City by Tuesday night. Wednesday saw us heading northeast on Interstate 44 from Oklahoma City through Tulsa and into the flatlands of St. Louis, Missouri.

We soon settled into a routine of driving twelve hours a day with brief stops for food and fuel. Allan didn't like driving on the "wrong" side of the road. Instead he took Caroline up on her offer of photography lessons and bought himself a digital camera in Tulsa. He must have shot several hundred images— mostly of cactus and sun-bleached gas stations with sleepy dogs out front. Herb always woke up to eat, and then check on the Swift before retiring again to his lair in the back seat of the truck. I didn't mind. He'd earned it.

Outside of throwing things at him during the night to temporarily stop his snoring, I didn't see much of Rick. He had been unusually quiet since stopping in Albuquerque. There he'd found a hobby shop and returned with a box-load of balsa wood, carving knives, glue, and sandpaper. He then locked himself in the back bedroom of the motor home where, I assumed, he spent long hours whittling away. What he was really up to became clear on Thursday morning. We stopped to gas up before picking up Interstate 55 north from St. Louis. As I pumped ninety gallons of diesel into the truck, I watched Rick step out of the motor home, and, carrying a cardboard box, climb the rear ladder onto the roof. He then proceeded to remove five small balsa wood constructions from the box, each about the size of a loaf of bread, and attach them firmly to the roof rack.

I finished fueling the Dodge, replaced the pump nozzle, and walked over. This looked strange, even for Rick.

"So, a new line of Christmas decorations?" I said.

Rick peered over the edge of the roof and smiled mysteriously. "Santa never had anything like these babies. Come on up and check it out."

I climbed the ladder and walked carefully across the motor home's roof to the spot where Rick was kneeling. He had attached five scale models of rear race-car wings across the front of the motor home's roof rack, each with dozens of miniature red streamers attached.

"So, this is what exactly?"

"This," Rick replied with obvious pride and excitement, "is a rolling aerodynamic test lab. I've spent the last two days on the laptop writing code and working out some new rear-wing designs for the Swift. It took me most of last night to build these five models. Each one is a different configuration. Once we're rolling, I'll be able to see how the air flows over them. I'll watch the streamers and see exactly how the air behaves as it passes over each wing. The new software I've written factors in the miniature size, and reduced speed of the motor home. And it compensates for air deflection from the windshield. I've even allowed for—"

I cut him off. "Hang on a second. Did you say you'd be able to watch them?"

Rick seemed even more excited about this part.

"Absolutely. This motor home is going to be like a rolling wind tunnel!"

I had some very serious doubts about this plan. Race car designers do build scale models of cars and wings, which they then take to a real wind tunnel for testing under strictly controlled conditions. They do not attach models to the roof of a road vehicle and drive down the interstate. I was about to point this out to Rick when it occurred to me that this could be a good thing. It would be much smarter all around if he kept himself busy, especially at night. I'd have to put up with his keyboard clicking away all night, but that was way better than the dry land snorkeling.

"OK, this might work," I replied evenly. "But the wings are on the roof and you'll be inside the motor home. What do you plan to do, hang yourself halfway out the window?"

Rick shook his head at my obvious stupidity.

"Eddie, please. That would be dangerous. No, I intend to do my observations properly. I'll strap myself down to the roof rack with bungee cords—behind the wings, of course, so as not to disturb the airflow."

"Excuse me?"

"It's simple, really. I'll just tie myself down and take my clipboard and some tools up there to make minor adjustments. I plan on using a couple of Caroline's cameras to take some video and pictures, too. Keep a visual record. What do you think?"

"I think some of that wood glue got up your nose and stuck all your brain cells together." It was Caroline, who stood peering over the top of the ladder.

She fixed Rick with a cold stare. "You are not riding to Milwaukee strapped to the roof with my cameras, Richard. Period."

"Well how can I do my observations, then?" he replied in frustration.

"You could always put another hole in the ceiling from inside. Right through, this time," I offered.

Rick was delighted.

"Hey, not bad, Eddie! Yeah. That might just work. There's a large square roof vent right behind the roof rack. I could remove the cover and the screen, stand on a box or something, and stick my head out. I can make my observations from there. Great idea!"

At Rick's insistence, Caroline and I stayed up top to remove the vent cover while he went inside the motor home to set up his observation post. When we climbed down and went in, I discovered that the "post" consisted of an ironing board with a folding lawn chair attached with duct tape.

"Perfect," Rick said, surveying his solution. I thought that he might have been safer strapped to the roof.

We set off on the last leg of our journey. We by-passed most of Chicago and arrived in Milwaukee early on a warm and muggy Thursday evening. Rick was determined to remain perched on his lawn chair the whole way, and he spent seven straight hours with his head stuck out of the motor home's roof, taking pictures, video and writing observations on his wing designs. He got more than a few odd looks from people in other cars as he grinned at them when they passed us. The monotony of this final day was broken briefly just outside of Chicago when a new, jet-black Porsche with Florida plates and a very dark window tint tailed us for a full half hour. It would come up alongside, drop back, and then close up again. Finally I waved it past and it blasted by and disappeared into the distance. Strange driving pattern but if you were traveling cross-country, that was definitely the way to do it.

Caroline had booked us into three large suites at the Miramar Motel, a huge sprawling complex with hundreds of rooms, four restaurants, a dinner theatre, two ballrooms and an Olympic-sized outdoor pool. We pulled into the far end of the parking lot, and emerged tired, stiff and relieved. Rick finally descended from his perch. He was beet red from the neck up from a serious case of sunburn, his blond hair was blasted straight back from the wind, and the sun had baked dozens of little smashed bugs on to the lenses of his glasses. Stretching and yawning, Herb walked slowly around Rick, examining him closely.

"Bad hair day?" he asked.

"Don't ask," Rick rasped through cracked lips.

We grabbed our luggage and met Caroline in the

lobby. With military precision, she registered every-one and passed out our keys. Herb and I had a suite next to Rick and Allan, with Sophie and Caroline just down the hall. We had a couple of hours until dinner, so we all unpacked and tried to unwind after four days on the road. Herb immediately went down to the trailer to check on the Swift, Rick and Allan went for the huge, outdoor pool, and Sophie and Caroline found the steam room. After four days in the truck, I needed to move. I pulled on my jogging gear, found a lakefront path, and went for a long run.

I got back in time for a quick shower and found a note from Herb telling me to meet them downstairs in the hotel's Chinese restaurant. When I arrived, they already had the menus out. Herb had gone back to the kitchen to see if they knew any oriental pancake recipes. It seemed like we ordered just about every-thing on the menu twice, but it didn't take long for us to empty the plates. Rick raved to Caroline and Sophie about the pool and insisted that they had to try it out, while Herb bravely hid his disappointment at the lack of pancakes by devouring three dozen spring rolls like he was eating popcorn. After dinner Caroline distributed our passes and schedules, and Allan went over our responsibilities. While no one actually said it, we all accepted that he would be the final authority on anything to do with the race car.

After a brief discussion with the waiter about whether or not it was humanly possible for anyone to consume three orders of spring rolls, Caroline paid the bill. Rick, Allan, and Herb went to the track to register, find our assigned pit area, and drop off our trailer. Sophie and Caroline rushed back to their room to watch *Swan Lake* on the Arts Channel, and I went to the room to study. This involved reading Allan's track notes on a laptop and then driving a computer simulation of the Milwaukee Mile on the computer. I had four races, crashed in three, and finished seventeenth in the other.

I decided to cut my losses and was asleep moments after my head hit the pillow

Chapter 8

The Wall

Friday morning came early for all of us. Showers and breakfasts were quickly out of the way, and we rolled out of the parking lot shortly after sunrise. We drove in the cool dawn air for half an hour across town to the Wisconsin State Fair Grounds.

The Milwaukee Mile was originally built almost 100 years ago for horse racing. It is one of the oldest racetracks in the world, and open-wheeled cars in one form or another have raced there since the twenties. The track is a true oval of exactly one mile in length, with four turns surrounded by foot-thick concrete walls. Unlike a road course, there's nowhere to go if you get it wrong. Making the slightest mistake in any one of the corners at the Mile will put you quickly and solidly into the wall.

Champ Cars can hit 175 miles per hour on the short

straights, stay close to that through the corners, and lap Milwaukee in well under 23 seconds. A good Atlantic car isn't much slower, getting down the straights at nearly 150 miles per hour and lapping in the high 20s.

I would have to adjust to the traffic on a short track, where someone would be passing or getting passed on almost every lap. I'd raced open-wheel shifter karts and formula cars for years, but my biggest challenge would be to adapt to racing on an oval—something I had never done before. The constant braking, shifting, and balancing of the car through a variety of corners required on a road or street course didn't apply here. At the Mile, you got up to speed and concentrated hard on staying there. And you remembered to turn left. Always.

We got through registration quickly with the other car owners and Atlantic racers. This was a little different crowd than I was used to. Most of the teams were young and with big-budget sponsors. To race in this series, they had come from Canada, Europe, Japan, and South America. And although I hadn't seen him yet, I knew that Raul DaSilva's outfit would be here. For over twenty years, the Formula Atlantic series had graduated drivers into Champ Cars, Indy cars, and even Formula One, and many of these drivers were here to launch a career. After picking up our passes, everyone went back quietly to our pit area to set up and prepare for our first practice session in the afternoon.

Except me. I did a nice interview with a guy from the local newspaper who really liked the idea of the underdog team from nowhere. I then walked through the pit infield in the middle of the track to have a closer look at my first oval. The corners were all of equal radius, slightly banked at nine degrees, and connected by two short straights. It all looked simple enough except for the presence of the thick, white, concrete wall that ringed the entire track. A mistake on a road course usually meant a fast trip through the grass or maybe a glancing blow off a guardrail. Get it wrong here, I told myself, and there would be none of that. I would meet the wall at close to 150 miles per hour. And there were several ugly black impact marks halfway up the wall in every turn—silent reminders of the price others before me had paid for their mistakes.

All of this was running through my head as I walked back to our pit. The Atlantic practice session was thirty minutes away, and despite the scarred wall, I couldn't wait. Rick climbed into the Swift. We hooked up a tow strap to a pit cart we'd rented, loaded it up with a toolbox, spare wheels and a jack, and set off for the "hot pits" at trackside. We towed the car through the crowds, and as soon as we arrived at trackside, I zipped up my new driving suit and stepped back to admire the gleaming red Swift. Caroline had added our new number, 28, to both sides in brilliant white numerals, along with the required signs and decals from the series sponsors. It was time to gear up. I put in earplugs, pulled on my flameproof hood, then the helmet and the HANS device—a brace that fit behind the helmet and acted as a head-and-neck restraint in case of an accident. I slid down into the driver's seat. Allan helped me buckle up the six-point harness and I pulled on my gloves. Rick had fitted an onboard radio system so that we could communicate throughout the race. Allan plugged a small cable from behind the roll bar into the side of my helmet, put on a headset, and switched on a transmitter clipped to his belt.

"Hello, Edward. How do you read?" he asked.

I pressed a small yellow button, labeled Transmit, on the steering wheel.

"Loud and clear, Allan. Man, this is loud. Sounds like you're right inside my helmet."

"Good. Once you're moving, it will be harder to hear. All right. First practice session in a new car and on a new track—and first time on an oval. What does that tell you?"

"That I'd better be careful."

"Agreed. And that starts with watching your mirrors. Expect to be passed. Constantly. Stay close to the wall on the straights and near the middle of each turn. Let the faster cars go low and inside. I want five nice, smooth laps to warm things up. Then I'll call you in and we'll check tire pressures and temperatures, and make sure everything's working properly."

"And then?"

Allan smiled. "And then, if I'm satisfied, you may begin to do some serious motoring."

I nodded. Allan flicked the master switch on, and in my mirrors I glimpsed Herb and Rick hooking up the remote starter battery. They locked it in, I spun the Cosworth engine over, and it barked to life, buzzing through the car with welcome vibrations. It was nothing like the thundering animal pulse of the Mustang's big V-8, but it sounded strong and a bit angry. I checked the alignment of my mirrors a final time. Allan stepped away from the front of the Swift and waved me out.

Rick and Herb gave me push to get rolling, I found first gear, brought up the engine revs, let out the clutch slowly, and tried to ease my way forward and smoothly out on to the pit lane.

And stalled it.

The guys pulled me back. They hooked up the battery and I restarted the engine. I gave it lots of throttle this time and briefly lit up both rear tires in a cloud of burning rubber as I streaked away. Then I had to hit the brakes hard to stay under the thirty-mile-per-hour speed limit in the pit lane. A real hot-dog move. Just the thing to impress your new race engineer.

I left the pit lane and was finally rolling as I quickly accelerated the Swift up through second and third gears, crossed the blend line at the end of the pit lane, entered turn one, and merged out onto the racetrack. The track surface was as smooth as glass, and it was great to be in an open-wheeled single-seat formula car again. Unlike the Mustang, the view ahead was completely clear. The Swift responded instantly to the slightest touch. The Cosworth twin-cam pulled hard. I built speed steadily, taking it up through fourth and then into fifth gear with the Swift feeling more stable the faster we went. For these first few laps I just circulated, letting everything come up to temperature and getting used to the lightness of the controls. And watching my mirrors. A few other cars were out as well, but none were near me. All too quickly it seemed Allan was on the radio.

His voice crackled inside my helmet. "Finish this lap and then in."

I flashed past Rick, who was holding out our pit board with IN written on it. Thanks, guys. Got it. I completed that lap, peeled off of turn four, entered the pit lane, and brought the Swift to a stop, engine running. Immediately Herb and Rick were buzzing around the car, checking and noting tire temperatures and pressures, body fasteners, and wing angles. Allan knelt beside the car and keyed his radio.

"How did it feel?"

"Great! Smooth and strong."

Allan shook his head, smiled, and pointed to the transmit button on the wheel. I held it down and repeated the message.

He nodded. "All right, then. This session is only thirty minutes, so it's time to get down to business. I want five laps, each slightly quicker than the last, then five more at a constant speed that feels comfortable."

I nodded and gave him a thumbs-up sign. With a push on the rear wing from Herb, the Swift was rolling. I accelerated out smoothly this time, leaving the pits and entering the track as before. Traffic was a factor now as most of the thirty cars entered seemed to be out. I got up to speed and concentrated on staying near the middle of the track and carving my line through the four turns as smoothly as possible. The Swift felt solid and the laps went by incredibly quickly. This seemed much easier than muscling the Mustang around a road course. I glanced over at Rick and was surprised to see him holding up the L6 sign. Four more steady laps and then in.

For the first time I glanced in my mirrors and saw a train of four cars bearing down on me fast. Leading the pack was Raul DaSilva's bright yellow car with its flashy stars and lightning-bolt paint job. I held my line. The pack swooped down the inside as one—and left me coming out of turn two as if I were driving Sophie's motor home in a school zone. No lap records for me today. Maybe going fast here wasn't as easy as it appeared.

Allan came on the radio. "Bring it in, Edward."

I pulled in, and again Rick and Herb were all over the car while Allan knelt down. I pushed up my visor to get some cool air.

"Everything OK?" I asked, remembering to push the transmit button this time.

"Fine. Temperatures look good, engine sounds happy. Settling in?"

"Sure. It's a very nice ride."

Allan raised an eyebrow.

"Well, we can't have that then, can we? You've got

about twelve minutes left. Get less comfortable. Push it a bit."

"Yes, sir!" I grinned. I snapped down my visor and left the pits with a touch of wheelspin.

The next ten laps flew by. I tried slightly different lines out of the corners and went gradually deeper into each one. I could feel the speed building at each lap, and a rhythm was starting to come as I settled into a pattern of throttle lift points and cornering lines. Rick held up a 2 MIN sign, indicating that the practice session was winding down. Most of the other cars had left the track, but I wanted to get in a few more laps and try a new, and I hoped quicker, entry into turn one.

I came down the grandstand straight with the throttle wide open, but instead of lifting, I kept my foot on the gas while I feathered the brake with my left. It was a technique I'd learned racing karts, and the Swift turned in well, flew through turn one, and carved hard into turn two. At first. Then without any warning the back end let go and the whole car snapped hard-right into a spin.

I nailed the brakes and locked all four wheels, but I knew that the wall was only a heartbeat away.

The impact came from behind as the rear wing bit into the concrete at the exit of turn two. It was less than I had feared—more like a hard jolt and nothing like the hit I took in the Mustang at Laguna. Still, it was more than enough to pitch the Swift violently to the left and into a series of spins toward the infield grass, where I eventually came to rest. Allan was on the radio instantly.

"Edward, are you all right?"

I just sat there, feeling exactly the same as I had after the Mustang accident at Laguna. Stupid. Clumsy. Embarrassed. I had done it again—pushed too hard and trashed two weeks of work in less than a second.

"Repeat. Eddie, are you all right?"

I pressed the transmit button.

"Yes, Allan. I'm OK."

"Good. Out you get, then, and we'll see you in a few minutes." He sounded relieved.

The marshal's truck arrived. I removed the steering wheel and was quickly helped to unbuckle and climb out of the car. I looked back to survey the damage. The rear wing was in pieces, scattered across the track. And judging by the angle of the right rear wheel, I had also done a fine job of bending the suspension. Half an hour in the car and I'd just bought the guys another all-nighter.

One of the marshals walked me back to the truck.

"Good thing you hit backward," he said.

I pulled off my helmet, stuffed my hood into it and yanked out my earplugs in frustration.

"Yeah? How's that?" I snapped.

"Guys who hit forward don't walk back to the truck."

Chapter 9

Silly Wings

Caroline, rewind it again back to—yeah, right there."

Rick had his nose inches from the laptop screen. The three of us had been squinting at it for almost an hour, watching my introduction to the Milwaukee Mile's north wall on video, frame by frame, over and over again. During practice, Caroline had set up her video camera on the roof and taped every lap we ran.

After watching the shiny red blur bounce off the concrete about thirty-five times, my eyes finally glazed over and my head slumped onto the dinette table.

"Rick, enough. This is sick. I can't watch it anymore," I moaned.

Caroline sat back and rubbed her eyes.

"Rick, he's right. I think we'd all be more use outside helping Herb and Allan, don't you?"

Rick wrote some more numbers and a string of question marks on a notepad, and stretched a kink out of his neck.

"Tell you what. You two go out and see how the repairs are going. There's something on this video I've missed."

"Missed?" I asked. "It's not a complicated story, Rick. Boy racer drives new car. Hits wall. Roll credits. The End."

I stood and made my way out the door with Caroline. Herb and Allan had the Swift up on waist-high work stands. They had removed the bodywork, and what was left of the smashed rear wing, and stripped the entire back end off the car. Parts and tools were scattered everywhere. Herb was busy with a drive shaft at a portable workbench while Allan was going through metal cases of spare parts.

"So?" I floated the question out to either of them.

Herb responded without looking up. "So, Allan. What do you suppose these two have been watching on that laptop for the past hour?"

Allan paused, considered this for a few long moments, and in a hushed tone replied, "Well, I can only imagine. Perhaps a romantic movie matinee?"

Herb nodded. "Chick flick on the laptop. I would-n't be surprised."

"Oh stop it!" Caroline snapped. "You two sound like a couple of old busybodies."

"Actually we were downloading recipes from *Pancakes dot-barf*," I added dryly. "We got you one for sweet-potato-and-chili-pepper flapjacks, Herb."

"Had those," Herb replied without looking up. "Too dry. They need a lot of syrup."

We walked around the Swift trying to get some idea of what was needed and how long the repairs might take. Allan joined us and pointed to a deep gash, about three inches long, ground crudely into the aluminum casing on the rear cover of the gear-box.

"This is where you nicked the wall after the right rear wheel and the wing hit. Another inch or two and you would likely have taken off the gearbox and we'd be looking for a complete new chassis as well. So the good news, Edward, is that we need only replace the gearbox cover, right rear suspension, drive shaft, and the rear wing assembly."

Caroline ran her fingers slowly over the scraped metal as if to soothe and heal a wound. She looked up at Allan.

"And the bad news?"

"It's going to take us all of today and into the early morning to put it right. Never mind. Could be worse. At least we know you were trying, Edward," Allan stated.

I had to agree, but what I also knew—and what no one needed to say—was that it could have been a whole lot better. The guilt still weighed heavily on me. I was supposed to be the driver, not the demolition guy.

"How can I help?" I asked.

Herb brought over the bent drive shaft and selected a new one from a spares box. "How about you guys go find out if there are any official practice times posted yet. We've got some times but it would be nice to know how fast everyone else is. I'm sure that the boss will put you to work when you get back," he said, smiling slyly at Allan.

Caroline and I left and made our way across the infield toward Race Control. For a change it was a short walk. We took time to pause and marvel at some of the huge transporters and dozens of crew members that the teams with big national sponsors had on display. I wondered if that level of financial backing and technical support really did make a difference on the track, or if most of it was just to impress everyone—especially the sponsors. I believed that a small and talented team like ours could do just as well as the teams with fat wallets. Provided I kept the car in one piece, I'd have a chance to test that theory tomorrow.

We reached Race Control and scanned a large bulletin board outside the timing office until we found a long sheet entitled *Friday Practice 1: Formula Atlantic*. Caroline pointed to the top.

"Here, Eddie. Look. Guess who? Mr. Personality himself."

Leading all entrants was number 4, Ascension Motorsports, Raul DaSilva, São Paulo, Brazil, with a time of 25.68 seconds.

Great. My favorite guy.

Even worse, the second-fastest car was Raul's teammate, number 3, Karl Heinrich, clocking in at 25.71 seconds. The rest of the thirty-two-car field was listed in a similar way, with the times gradually lengthening into the 26- and 27-second range. I ran my finger down the list until I found my name, entered by Novello Racing, Aunt Sophie's new business. Then I saw my time: 28.89 seconds. Dead last.

"This is a disaster, Caroline."

She looked puzzled. "So you're a couple of seconds behind the fast guys. Couldn't you make that up in the race?"

I shook my head. "At this rate I won't even quali-fy. There are thirty-two cars entered and only twen-ty-eight will make the cut. Even if I make it in, I'm still three seconds per lap slower than Raul's time. That's nowhere. I mean, say we both raced at these speeds. He'd be catching and passing me about every nine laps. Over a sixty-lap race, I'd eventually finish six or seven laps behind DaSilva."

Caroline bit her lip as she confirmed the math. "You're right. Man, that would be embarrassing. Well, let's just make sure that you find three seconds before qualifying tomorrow. Come on."

We walked back to our pit silently, each occupied with our own thoughts about how we could shave my time of 28.89 down at least into the 26-second range—and how it would feel if we couldn't.

"Stewart!"

The nasally voice came from behind me and to the left. I stopped. I knew even before I turned that it was Raul. He strutted over, dressed in a bright yel-low polo shirt, perfectly-tailored black slacks, and a pair of $500 shoes. On each arm he had a very tall and very pretty girl, both of whom looked like they'd stepped right out of a fashion show.

"Raul DaSilva," I said flatly.

"Ah, yes. Eddie Stewart." He looked me over

from head to toe, inspecting, comparing—satisfying himself that he was superior.

"You are surprised that I remember you," he said.

"We didn't exactly part on the best of terms, Raul."

He gave me the hawk smile.

"No. That was an unfortunate scene with Tanner. That will all be put right in time; you may depend upon it. But it is over now, and as for today, life is fantastic, no? I am fastest in practice. My teammate is second. And I have my two companions."

His dark, predatory eyes bored straight into Caroline's. "And I am this moment gazing upon a vision of rare beauty. Where are your manners, Stewart?"

"Raul DaSilva, meet Caroline Grant," I said coldly.

I felt as if Caroline was about to step in something awful and that I should do something to protect her.

"*Enchanté, Mademoiselle,*" Raul announced in flawless French. "A singular pleasure, Caroline."

Caroline met his gaze and smiled thinly. "Please, call me Miss Grant. So you're Raul DaSilva. I've heard of you."

"No doubt," Raul replied with practiced conceit.

Caroline didn't bite. "You were very fast this morning," she said pleasantly.

"Yes, it is true. I am fastest. Again. But then this is

expected of the series leader."

Raul turned his gaze to me.

"So, now you hope to drive in Formula Atlantic, Stewart. Quite a step up. You seemed to be struggling out there—even found the wall in turn two, I am told. But then this is your first race at this level, and you are new to professional competition. I will give some advice. You should be careful. You will quickly find that to compete with us takes more than the kindness of your friends. And some silly wings."

That was odd. Silly wings? Rick had his new wing models locked away in the motor home, and he hadn't yet finished building a full-sized wing to his new specs. How could Raul possibly know anything about that?

"Thanks for the tip, Raul. I'll be all right. We might even surprise you," I said evenly.

Raul checked his gold Rolex watch, and considered the possibility for a few seconds.

"Somehow I doubt it. A delight to meet you, Caroline. I look forward very much to seeing you again."

Raul turned with the models and swept back down the pit lane.

"Definitely something slimy about that guy," Caroline stated as we walked back to our pit. I simply nodded and smiled, admiring her excellent judge of character.

Chapter 10

Making the Show

We found Rick seated at a work table buried in diagrams and calculations, energetically explaining something to Herb and Allan. We listened in as he detailed how he had at last found what he was looking for on the tape—video evidence that the car had become rapidly unstable, losing rear grip as I had turned into the second turn on my final lap.

Losing the back of the car is technically termed *oversteer*, where the rear end suddenly loses grip and snaps around in a slide. Oval drivers just use the word "loose," and while this setup could work to your advantage in tight corners on a road or street course, it is absolutely the worst thing to have on an oval.

At a place like Milwaukee you want the opposite:

understeer, or "push," where the front end gradually starts to slide before the back. That situation can usually be fixed by easing off the throttle slightly until the front tires find their grip again and the car regains its line and exits the corner safely. With oversteer, however, the back of a car drifts out sideways, and trying to correct that sort of slide on an oval almost always guarantees a fast trip into the wall.

"Here, look. I've enhanced and enlarged this sequence. Now watch frame by frame," Rick said.

He directed our attention to the laptop screen. I watched as the Swift turned in then suddenly snapped sideways halfway through the turn. Even in freeze frame it was alarming. Allan whistled and slowly looked up at me.

"A bit of a shock, Edward?"

"It got my full attention."

"Still, you held it well. The damage could have been more severe."

Allan looked over at Rick. "So, Richard. The problem…and your solution?"

This was just like judging at the national science fair, which Rick had won twice in high school. He loved it.

"The problem is a sudden loss of grip, most likely caused by insufficient downforce from the rear wing.

It is basically an aerodynamic problem," Rick stated with certainty.

"Downforce? I thought the back wing just stopped the car from taking off," said Caroline.

"Not really," Rick replied. "Its main job is to create negative lift, or downforce, to push the whole car down onto the track. The bodies on these cars also have trays underneath and tunnels on each side that direct the airflow straight back to the wing. That's what allows them to blast through the turns almost without slowing down. Obviously, the wing couldn't generate enough downforce to hold the car at the speed Eddie had it up to entering the turn. And since that wing it is now in all these little tiny pieces, the solution is clear. We need a new rear wing. And I just happen to have a design ready."

Allan stroked his close-cropped beard thoughtfully and then nodded in agreement.

"Excellent," Rick chirped.

Caroline wasn't so sure. "Rick, I of all people know how brilliant you are and everything, but will your new design really be any better? Balsa wood models on the motor home roof moving at 60 miles per hour isn't quite the same thing as full scale on this oval at 160. And with your best friend sitting in front of it."

"Fair enough," Rick replied. "There's always some

risk with anything new. But I think it's acceptable. I've written a software simulation for it and run the calculations a dozen times. By the numbers, this design should generate seventeen to twenty-two per-cent more downforce than the original wing without affecting straight-line speed. So, around Milwaukee, that should clip a full two seconds per lap off our best time." It was just about what I needed to go from the back of the field to somewhere near the front.

Herb held up his extra-large hand. "Excuse me. Hello? One minor point, guys. Where is this marvel of technology? All we have is your nice little model and a spare standard wing in the trailer."

Rick was already up and shouting from inside the trailer as he retrieved the spare.

"No problem! We can use some of the spare stan-dard wing and I've already made the pieces we need to modify it to my new design. Couple of hours tops, and we're in business for qualifying tomorrow."

It took fourteen hours.

Between cutting, fitting, shaping, riveting, and welding Rick's new pieces, and repairing the crash damage, we all worked flat out until 2:00 a.m., when Caroline and Sophie finally sent me back to the motel. They reasoned that if anyone was to be awake tomorrow it had better be the guy strapped in behind the wheel.

I couldn't argue that point, but I still couldn't drift off. After about three hours of tossing and turning, I gave up. I showered and changed, and then grabbed some breakfast and drove back to the track through the quiet, sleepy streets. I found our pit deserted, but the Swift sat quietly, fully assembled, with the polished aluminum of Rick's new wing gleaming in the cool morning light.

I tried creeping quietly into the motor home but found everyone at various stages of waking up, stumbling to the shower, and trying to clear the haze out of their heads. Our qualifying session was at 10:00 a.m., and by 9:00 we were feeling mostly human again. With the addition of our new wing, the car had to go through technical inspection again; Herb took Rick with him to get that done.

Spirits improved greatly when Sophie announced that we could at last wear our new official crew uniforms. I was sure that we all looked like something the cat dragged in, but with lots of Herb's "real" coffee, some aspirin, dark sunglasses, and snappy new uniforms, we were ready to face the day.

Again, it grew hot, sunny, and humid—good for spectators and racing engines, and to get the slick tires working at high temperature. But the heat was always hard on drivers, especially a rookie with no sleep in a new car. Rick and Herb put Allan's Milwaukee CD in the laptop and checked the Swift's suspension against his specs, while I met with him to discuss qualifying strategy. The approach was similar to yesterday's practice, but with less time.

In this series, Formula Atlantic qualifying on an oval track was one car at a time, four timed laps each, with the field split into two groups based upon practice times. It was up to me to push as hard as I could in those laps and set a qualifying time which would at least get us into the afternoon race. Appropriately, I lined up dead last in the "slow" group session. It

seemed to take forever. The fifteen guys ahead of me all did their qualifying runs before I was finally waved out.

Herb fired the engine, they pushed me out, and I did two warm-up laps carefully, making sure everything was working properly, and feeling the car out after the crash. If anything, it felt tighter. I made a quick call to Allan on the radio and took the green flag to start my qualifying run. The only thing on my mind was to qualify this car somewhere, anywhere, on the starting grid. I had to make the show.

I had four laps to set a time. Starting my first qualifying lap, I gradually unleashed the Swift. Immediately I noticed that it was much more stable than in practice, especially through the four equal corners where it seemed quite happy to take just about any line. It had to be Rick's wing. The rhythm of acceleration, lift points, and turn in angles came back quickly, and I found that I was able to go deeper into the corners and get on the gas sooner coming out of them. If anything, the car wanted more speed, and I almost felt as if I was holding it back. Allan came on the radio as I entered the back straight.

"Everything OK?"

"Excellent! You guys built me a race car! Tell Rick!"

"He knows. Focus now, Edward."

For the second lap I held the throttle to the floor as I eased my left foot over the brake pedal going into turn one. I was about to try the same move that had put me into the wall yesterday, but I felt that this time I had the car under me to do it. And it was definitely faster.

Left-foot braking is basically a kart racing technique where the driver rolls off the gas slightly with the right foot and brakes with the left at the same time while entering a corner, and then reverses the process coming out of it. Done smoothly on an oval where you don't need to downshift, it's far less upsetting to the car; and it can get you into and out of a corner carrying some serious speed. Still, the memory of yesterday's impact was still fresh, and I had to force myself to keep my foot in the throttle.

Unlike yesterday, the Swift bit into the corners immediately, stayed flat, and the G-forces pushed me hard against the side of the cockpit. I actually found it difficult to hold my head level through the corners. Either I was weak from lack of sleep or this thing was really flying.

The remaining qualifying laps were over in a blur and the checkered flag waved. I coasted back into our pit anxious to get the answer. They knew even before I rolled to a stop and shut off the engine. They stood in line in their bright new uniforms and, with bright new smiles, held up their index fingers.

I released my harness and unplugged the radio connector. I levered myself quickly out of the car and pulled off my neck brace, helmet, and hood. Still they didn't move. Just stood there, grinning, with their fingers pointing up.

"So, is this some rude English thing with the finger, Allan?"

"Can you count, Edward?" he replied.

I counted. One. Number 1. Fastest session qualifier. Duh. I got it.

They read the expression on my face, and the celebrating began. Slaps on the back, handshakes (except with Herb), high-fives, and low-fives. Rick—as Elvis again—climbed into the car for the tow back to our pit area with his arms spread wide, drawling, "Well, thankya. Thankya vera much!"

On the short ride back, a beaming Caroline handed me her clipboard. Lap one was in the high 26-second range, decreased quickly to a low 26 for lap two, and finished with two laps in the 25s. My best time was a 25.58 seconds, faster even than Raul DaSilva's time yesterday. I still must have looked stunned, so after we rolled the Swift back into our pit, Allan sat me down at a table, filled two tall glasses with ice, and poured us some of Sophie's limeade.

Allan clinked his glass against mine and raised it in salute. "Well done, Edward. Very well done indeed."

"I still can't believe it. We led the second group's session."

"We did. More precisely, you did. First time on an oval. First time in Atlantics. Quite amazing, really."

"The car was amazing."

"Yes, it looked very strong. As you did. A very nice touch behind the wheel those last two laps."

"Thanks. So where are we now, Allan? Front row? Pole position?"

Allan laughed and rubbed his tired eyes. "No, probably not on the pole. Not yet, anyway. The fast group is out next, and they will be quicker than yesterday. We'll have to wait and see what their times are—especially DaSilva and Heinrich. And the Frenchman, Stefan Veilleux, has been fast. He'll bear watching, too. But I do think that when that green flag drops this afternoon, there won't be many ahead of you."

Chapter 11

Focus

As it turned out, Allan was right. The "fast" group didn't get that label for nothing. They all looked like they were under the lap record, and when the final times were posted, two of them actually were. As usual, Raul DaSilva and his teammate, Karl Heinrich, led the field in the low 25s. My time of 25.58 seconds had held up, however. I was slated to start fifth out of twenty-eight qualifiers. For someone who was worried about making the race a day earlier, I certainly couldn't complain.

As the Atlantic cars were again the preliminary show with the Champ Cars as the main event, scheduling was tight. Our race was set to go in two hours. Caroline and Sophie set up shop on the motor home's roof. Herb, Rick, and Allan went over every inch of the Swift to make sure it was fully prepped for sixty laps.

Given the fact that I hadn't really slept for a day and a half, I thought that the best thing I could do was stretch out in the motor home and rest my eyes for a few minutes.

An hour and a half later I woke up to the chorus of "Viva Las Vegas"—as usual, performed by Rick but with backup this time from Caroline and Sophie. Actually, the girls sounded pretty good.

"What time is it?" I asked, sitting up and squinting.

"It is time for you to repay my investment," Sophie replied. "I am very excited to watch you drive the racing car now, Eddie."

"Ten minutes, ace. Suit up and we'll see you on the grid," Rick announced as the three of them left me to pull on three layers of flameproof driving suit.

The afternoon temperature had climbed into the nineties, which would mean a track surface temperature of well over 110 degrees. As it was going to be another sauna inside the car, I drank a full quart of mineral water before stepping out into the brilliant sun. I grabbed my helmet bag and trudged to the starting grid, wondering if we should consider ice racing in Finland next year.

I found the guys doing final checks on the Swift on the third row of the grid. Strangely, someone had covered our new rear wing with a large blue tarp, which only served to attract curious glances from other drivers and crews. I placed my helmet bag inside the car and turned to Allan.

"What's with the cloak-and-dagger stuff?" I asked, pointing to the covered wing.

Allan smiled. "Too many prying eyes and cameras for my liking. Rick's given us an advantage, and I plan to keep it for as long as we can. The tech inspectors have approved the new wing, and our competitors will eventually try to copy it. No sense putting it on display for them before we have to."

Rick said nothing—just beamed at the vote of confidence from Allan Tanner, Race Engineer. He and Herb proudly stood guard behind the car. I was about to pull on my gear and climb in when another driver came over, grinned broadly, and extended his hand.

He was maybe five and a half feet tall, with large ears, a nose to match, and a deep tan. Two sparkling black eyes and a cheeky grin were framed by a wild mass of curly black hair. More than anything, he looked like an elf. A racing elf.

"Eedie Stewart?" The elf asked in a thick accent. Not Eddie. *Eeeedie*. I shook his hand.

"That's right." I read the name on his driver's suit. "And you are Stefan Veilleux?"

I think I pronounced it more or less like *Steve Value*,

which probably sounded to him as bad as *Eeeedie* did to me.

"*Oui*. Yes. I am he, Stefan. I am a pleasure for meeting you."

SteFAHN. Ah, French. I suddenly regretted dropping French in grade ten.

"Good to meet you, too," I said. And I meant it. Stefan was instantly likable—and given that he was starting just ahead of in me third spot, obviously a quick race driver as well.

"I am for congratulating this to you, Eedie. Also, I am for congratulating your team. You are new here but good, I think." Stefan struggled with English but his meaning was clear.

"Thanks. Um, *merci*." I remembered that much.

"*Bonne chance*, Eedie! The luck, she is good." He waved and left me to get into his own car.

The luck, she is good. OK then.

An official held up the Five Minutes sign, which was the cue for all drivers to get in their cars. I pulled on my helmet and brace. With some help from Rick, I strapped in, pulled on my gloves, and tested radio communication with Allan. At the One Minute sign, we fired the engine and were soon rolling down the pit lane and out onto the Milwaukee Mile for the first of two warm-up laps behind the pace car.

For the very first time, I noticed the crowd. There were stands all the way around the track and they seemed to be full. On a road course, the crowds were usually spread out all around the circuit, but on a short oval it was almost like being on the field inside a huge football stadium. We did two fairly slow laps to warm the tires. We watched the pace car pull off, and then we began a third lap, where the front-row guys, DaSilva and Heinrich, would bring the field up to racing speed, keep the rows in order, and then cross the line rolling to take the green flag.

The Swift felt smooth, strong, and impatient. With only four cars in front of me, I had a great view of the starter's tower; and as we came out of turn four, he waved the green flag and sent a wave of twenty-eight shrieking Atlantic cars hammering into the first turn.

Raul led Heinrich, and I took a tight line to hold down fifth as we came through turns one and two, building speed down the back straight. Stefan Veilleux's blue car was in third, and ahead of me was an orange car with some cheese company sponsorship (It's Beddar with Cheddar!) on the rear wing.

The scheduled race distance was sixty miles, sixty laps. Allan had directed me to use the first ten to get into a rhythm, hold my top-five place and stay close to the leaders. We were lapping smoothly in the

26-second range, and after about five minutes, Allan came over the radio.

"Looking good, Eddie. Looking good. Lap eleven. Place five."

"Feels strong," I replied.

"Look for an opening. Make a move."

I had actually been holding back a little. I squeezed the throttle and held it wide open until I was right under the rear wing of the cheddar cheese car. I used his slipstream to pick up some more speed and then darted out from behind, drew level with him on the inside entry to turn one, and took fourth place as we exited on to the back straight. The lead group was just entering turns three and four, so I figured I had about a seven-second gap to make up.

The Swift pulled away from Mr. Cheese easily, carving the Milwaukee turns like it was on rails, and eating up the straights. I could see the gap to third shortening with every lap.

"Lap twenty. Place four. Gap is six. Repeat. Gap, six."

Thanks, Allan. I usually knew my place and had an idea of how far back I was. But I rarely had a clue which lap we were on.

I was part of the lead pack now, right behind Stefan Veilleux in third, then Heinrich, and finally Raul in the lead. This was shaping up very nicely. I planned to tail Stefan for a few laps, try and get him going into turn one, then deal with Karl and finally Raul. Lots of time.

"Yellow! Yellow! Yellow!"

I immediately lifted off the gas and checked my mirrors. Allan's shouting in my earphone meant that there had been an incident somewhere, and the officials were waving yellow flags all around the track, placing the entire field under a full-course caution. I couldn't see anything wrong behind me or in front.

It wasn't until we got onto the back straight that I understood why we were under yellow. It began with small, white pieces of smashed bodywork all over the track. Then I passed a rear wheel, which had been torn off with the suspension still attached. Then half of a front wing.

Finally, as we slowly entered turn three in single file, I saw two cars tangled together, up against the concrete wall. Oil and water oozed from the crash site, slowly running down the banking of the corner to the infield.

Five marshals had already crossed the track and were directing us to stay low and away from the wall as they dealt with the accident. I couldn't see the drivers, but it looked bad. I said a quick prayer of thanks, offered up another one for the drivers, and then radioed Allan. At cruising speed it was much easier to talk.

"Allan. What happened?"

"Two midfield cars got together. Watched it on the TV replay. Nasty."

"Are they OK?"

"Marshals have one of them. He's walking around. They're still working on the other."

"Should I pit?"

"NO! Form up behind the pace car. Stay out. Don't run over anything. Stay calm."

Right. Stay calm.

We cruised past the crash site again, and this time I took a closer look. I shouldn't have, but I did. An ambulance and four marshals were now on the scene, and they appeared to be using tools to cut into one of the cars to free a trapped driver. The stream of fluids from the crushed car continued to run down the track like blood from an open wound. Suddenly it wasn't too hot anymore.

Stay calm.

I hit the transmit button again. "Allan!"

"Go ahead, Edward."

"What do we do?"

There was a long pause. Allan sensed the tension in my voice.

"Edward, listen to me now."

"OK, go!"

"You look straight ahead—nowhere else. You check your dash display. You count laps. You listen to the car. You think about moving up. Can you do that?"

In other words, don't look over when you go by. Don't wonder. Don't think about what if it had been me trapped inside that wreck.

"Repeat. Can you do that, Edward?"

This time it was my turn to pause. I took a few deep breaths.

"I can do that."

"Good. You have to. Focus on what you can control—not on what you can't."

I tried. There was nothing to do but cruise around single file and wait. And for the next twelve laps (I counted every one), it worked to ease the fear. The radio was quiet. Each time past the scene I just watched the Swift's nose, my two front tires, and Stefan Veilleux's rear wing. I didn't look over at the ambulance finally rushing away, or at the tow truck picking up what was left of the cars, or at the marshals as they swept powdered cement, called Quick Dry, over the spilled fluids so that the racing could continue. Finally, the pace car's lights went off.

Allan came on instantly. "Going green in one lap. Green in one lap."

Chapter 12

Closing the Gap

As the pace car pulled off, DaSilva led the field single file through turns three and four, past the accident site, and back up to racing speeds. He was already hard on it before we got the green flag again, and started to pull out a new lead. We hadn't gone green but I nailed the throttle anyway. I needed the speed—the rush, the demand of instant decisions to clear my head. Focus on what you control.

The starter finally waved the green flag, and I was catching Veilleux fast as we crossed the line. I rushed up behind. Stefan went low, so I went high and to the right as we swept side by side into turn one. It was wheel to wheel, inches apart, with Stefan on my left and the dull white concrete wall rushing closer on my right, with a narrowing tunnel of open track ahead.

This was not the best place to be at 140 MPH. All Stefan would have to do was flick his steering wheel a fraction to the right, or drift up out of his inside line, and I'd be in the wall. Instantly. Someone had to lift off, and at this point I knew it couldn't be me. I was in too deep, committed to the high racing line with nowhere else to go.

Stefan knew it too.

At the last moment he lifted, slowing his car just enough to prevent us touching. I came off the turn a bit too high. The Swift twitched once dangerously but held the arc, and I took third as we rocketed together onto the back straight. In that moment I learned to trust the tiny Frenchman, who had done the smart and sportsmanlike thing by giving me some racing room. I knew it was more than Raul would have given me.

Heinrich was next. He was close—maybe twenty feet ahead—and Stefan and I were both catching him quickly. Almost too quickly. Stefan was right behind, tucked up under my rear wing. I was close enough to Heinrich to see him glance rapidly in his mirrors to see which way I would go. I remembered where I'd seen this blocking move from him before at Laguna Seca. Only this time I was no spectator.

"Lap thirty-seven. Place, three. Gap is one. Gap, one. "

Thank you, Allan. I wished he could radio Heinrich and tell him to get out of the way.

Stefan and I were all over Heinrich now. But he was just fast enough on the straights to stop us pulling alongside to pass, and he made sure that he took up all of the best racing line in every corner. If I couldn't pull him on the straights, I'd have to go dangerously low or high in the corners to try and get past. Or just be content to stay there and eventually let Raul build a lead no one could challenge. The laps went by and my frustration grew.

"Lap forty-four. Place, three. Gap, one. "

"Allan, he's blocking!"

"Be patient, Edward. Let him come to you. Focus."

Sixteen laps left. Eight minutes. I didn't like third. With Rick's wing gluing the Swift to the track, I knew I had the best-handling car in the race. But I was jammed up.

"Lapped traffic ahead! Use the traffic, Edward!" Allan shouted.

Allan was watching the race on a pit TV monitor, and he had seen the opportunity developing before I did. Raul had just gone by a group of four slower cars, putting them down a lap. We came up on them next.

As the leader of our pack, Heinrich would have to find a way to thread his car through them without slowing down too much—while also keeping me at bay. Heinrich knew that Stefan and I would follow him straight through. Allan was hoping that Heinrich would guess wrong and get blocked by a slower car, creating an opening for me to squeeze past. And with four cars ahead, the chances were good that someone was going to get in the way.

If it came, I knew that the opening would only be there for a second.

On the front straight I slipped up into position right underneath Heinrich's wing, my front nose cone less than a foot from the back of his gearbox. Sure enough, he began to slow as he looked for a way through the pack of slower cars ahead. The first two were paying attention to their mirrors and they both went low and to the left. Heinrich passed them high and to the right with me and Stefan right behind.

No chance there.

It took another full lap to catch the next two just going into turns one and two. A pass here would be more difficult unless the slower cars moved high or low out of the usual racing line. Heinrich was waiting for them to do one or the other, but they didn't. Both kept firmly to the racing groove, as if we weren't even there.

Halfway through the corner I decided that if

Heinrich was just going to sit and wait, I wasn't. I knew I had the handling and downforce to go low. I flicked the Swift to the left, swooping down and inside, inching forward until I was alongside—even with Heinrich's nose—and then pulling ahead as we came out of the turn. He was boxed behind two slower cars with me on his inside, pulling away.

Second place.

Allan was right there in my ear. "Well done, Edward! Lovely! Place, two. Fourteen laps. Fourteen laps. Gap is ten. Gap is ten."

The gap ahead to Raul was just ten seconds. That's all I needed to know. Ten seconds doesn't sound like much, but at the Milwaukee Mile it's almost half a lap. I could barely see his car ahead. It's always easier to hunt someone down when you can see the gap ahead shrinking—and when the guy you're catching sees you getting larger in his mirrors every lap. I checked my mirrors and saw that Stefan had also found a way past Heinrich and had his bright blue car a few seconds behind mine in third.

Ten seconds in fourteen laps. That's what I had to make up. With a clear track ahead, a light fuel load, and Rick's wing, I had a shot at pulling it off. I put in five laps right on the limit, using a little less left-foot braking and taking a higher line through the corners, which got me out onto the straights more quickly each lap.

"Nine laps. Gap is six. Repeat: nine laps. Gap, six."

Raul's bright yellow car was still a distant blip, but I was gaining. We were separated by about the length of a straightaway. I kept up the pace, calculating that I'd be up with him with maybe two laps left. I tried not to think about how sweet it would feel to go by him. Then I reminded myself that it would be one thing to catch someone like DaSilva, and quite another to pass him.

"Gap is 3. Three laps. Gap 3. Three laps."

I could see him clearly now, maybe fifty feet ahead. Raul had sped up, no doubt on radio instructions from his own crew. His car looked twitchy, nervous— right on the edge. Then I glanced ahead of his car and saw exactly what I needed.

Traffic.

I reeled him in quickly on the next lap as he slowed up to approach a group of slower cars, and we both got by them low and inside.

"Two laps, Edward. Focus. Two laps."

Thanks, Allan. But at that point I didn't care what lap it was. I was on him now and knew I was faster. I tailed Raul closely for a lap, watching his line—sometimes easing out from behind to his left, sometimes to his right. I wanted him nervous, watching his mirrors—wondering where I was, where I might go next—and splitting his concentration. It's a lot harder to lead than to pursue. I was counting on the mounting pressure to give me an opening.

We took the white flag signaling the final lap.

Last chance.

I knew Raul would stay low or in the middle groove, protecting his lead, using up as much of the track as possible in an attempt to block any passing move I might try. I decided, going into turn one for the final time, that I'd show him a move low and to the inside; and then if he went for it, I'd quickly snap the Swift up high and take him on the exit. It was the same move I'd used to get by Stefan earlier.

Raul DaSilva took the bait for my low inside move and, as I expected, slid his car down to block me going into turn one. At that instant, I immediately went for the high outside groove, looking for the narrowing gap between his car on my left and the concrete wall rushing past on my right. And it almost worked.

I forgot that while Raul was fast, he was no sportsman. The moment he realized that he'd lost me in his mirrors and that I wasn't really coming in low, he moved his car up into the high groove to close the gap. Slam the door. He knew I was there. He also knew that I would have to choose between locking wheels with him or getting crushed against the wall.

No thanks. I took the third choice. I had to back right out of the throttle and brake slightly. Even so, by then we were just too close, and we were going to get together at 140 miles per hour.

Raul's rear tire clipped the nose of the red Swift, ripping it and the front wing clean off the front of my car, sending it flashing over my head in three pieces. The impact cut deeply into the side of Raul's tire; and it instantly disintegrated, snapping his car sideways in front of me.

I braced myself for impact inside the Swift's cockpit, but it didn't come. We were both way out of control—tire smoke and wreckage filling the air. Then everything just seemed to slide into slow motion.

Raul's car spun slowly up toward the wall, I pulled to the left, and a chunk of tire took off my right side mirror. But somehow, by inches, I missed him. He slowly disappeared to my right. Incredibly, I found myself looking ahead at a clear track.

I snapped the Swift down two gears and accelerated hard down the back straight. I'd lost a ton of speed, and without a nose or front wing assembly anymore, I knew that the Swift wouldn't stick at all in the last two corners. I checked my remaining left-side mirror. No one close. I was almost up to normal straight-line speed again, but I had to back right off for turns three and four. Without any front wing, the car wanted to push straight ahead.

"Stay low! Stay low! Traffic right!"

Allan had seen what I no longer could. It was Heinrich, howling past on my blind right side as we exited for the last time onto the main straight. I tucked in behind him but knew it was over. His fist punched out of the cockpit as he took the checkered flag for the win—two seconds ahead of me.

I backed off the throttle and flipped up my helmet visor, drinking in the blast of cool, fresh air as I coasted through turns one and two. Stefan came alongside, excitedly pumping both his gloved hands up and down like pistons. I waved back. Heinrich also slowed, came alongside on my right, and gave me a thumbs-up. I waved back at him, too.

We cruised the back straight three abreast, waving to each other and to the crowd, who were on their feet clapping and cheering wildly. They'd come to see some close racing and we'd provided quite a show. I hit the radio.

"Hey, Allan! Now can I come in?"

"Yes, now is a good time. An excellent drive,

Edward! Bring it home. Hang on…. Just a minute."

There were banging and scratching noises over the radio—and then a new, very loud and very excited voice blasted inside my helmet.

"Eddie! Where are you? Talk to me!"

Aunt Sophie.

"Hi, Sophie! I'm in the car. Where else would I be?"

"Of course you are! Yes! In the car! Never mind. Did you have fun? Were you frightened? How is the car? Can we fix it? What do you want to eat? I have made—"

I had to cut in. "Sophie!"

"What?"

"Relax! I'm coming in. Right now."

"Good! We are here!"

"Yeah, I figured. I'll talk to you in about a minute."

"Yes! I will tell the others! Allan! Eddie is here! On the phone! He is coming into the thing here…the pit! This pit! Eddie, Allan says he already knows! What? Yes, Rickie. OK…no, do not start! No singing! Yes, Caroline, I know he is! OK! Just wait a—"

"Sophie!"

"What?"

"What's going on there?"

"No one is letting me talk."

"You don't need to talk to me on the radio. Calm

down. I'm turning into the pit lane now. I'll be there in a few moments."

"I know! OK! Nice to talk to you! Bye-bye now! Drive safely!"

Chapter 13

Podium Behavior

I didn't make it back to our pit. At least not right away. In the frantic excitement of those last few laps and my bizarre radio conversation with Sophie, it had somehow slipped my mind that I had finished second. That meant that the Swift went to the winner's circle area, where it would be impounded and inspected. This was standard procedure for the top three at any pro Atlantic race—to ensure that no one was running a car that was grossly underweight or that had a rocket engine tucked away somewhere out of sight. It also meant that, for the first time in my new professional career, I would be on the podium as one of the top three finishers.

As I wheeled into the pit lane, I was directed to park between the cars of Karl Heinrich and Stefan Veilleux, who were already unstrapped, climbing out, and congratulating each other. While I shut the engine down, removed my helmet, and stepped out, Stefan was waiting.

"Eedie! We are *fantastique!*" he yelled, spreading both arms wide.

"Stefan! I owe you one, man! You could have put me into the wall."

"Never! I am not the man, such as I am, who would do that thing to you. What racing you have today! Your car, she is *magnifique!*"

Even battle-scarred and missing its nose section, the liquid red Swift still looked lean, fast, and ready to take on all comers for another sixty laps. Not me, though. I was hot, sweat-soaked, dog-tired, and done in.

Almost reluctantly, Heinrich slowly walked over and joined us. For a guy who had just won the race, I thought that he looked worse than I felt. His blond hair was so closely cropped that he almost looked bald, and for a racing driver he was unusually tall and slim—built like a marathon runner. He'd seemed pretty happy inside his car on the victory lap, so I thought it strange that now he didn't look at all happy or relieved—or even just a little bit pleased with himself. Instead, he looked distracted and worried. He avoided making eye contact as he shook my hand.

"Good job, Stewart."

"Thanks. You too." Then I remembered the accident. And DaSilva. "Any word on the two guys who hit the wall?"

Heinrich seemed surprised by the question. "Apparently they're fine. Just shook up."

"And what about Raul? Did he finish?"

Heinrich wiped his face with a wet towel, supplied by a marshal.

"My crew told me Raul finished ninth. Out of the points. I have not talked to him yet," he said, turning away.

Heinrich actually looked depressed. Well, excuse me, I thought. I was having a hard time feeling sorry for poor Mr. DaSilva. I knew that Raul needed to score points in every race to keep his lead in the series championship, but you don't do that by driving like a maniac. If he lost the lead and put himself out trying to punt me off, then he deserved exactly what he got. I figured that ninth was about right. And anyway, his teammate went on to win. So why the long face from Heinrich?

The three of us were escorted to the base of the track control tower, placed on the podium, and handed some large, heavy trophies. Stefan and I hoisted Karl Heinrich's arms above his head in a victory salute to the crowd. Dozens of press cameras clicked.

There's your sports page shot, guys.

Then we were each presented with huge, silver dairy cans of ice-cold milk. Not champagne. Milk. After all, we were in Wisconsin, the Dairy State. I was just glad it wasn't a grilled cheese sandwich. I started to take a sip from mine, but Stefan had been on the podium before. He knew what to do.

He got Karl full in the face with the first blast from his milk can. I ducked under the second one aimed at me, but he still dumped the rest of his milk in my hair and down the front of my driving suit. I immediately returned fire with my own can, but Stefan was too quick. Instead, I caught the Race Queen square in the back. Shrieking, she in turn grabbed Karl's milk can, and got me in the face.

From there, it was open warfare. Drivers, officials, marshals, the Race Queen, press guys—it didn't matter. Anything liquid was ammo, and for a few minutes the victory presentation had rapidly turned into a cafeteria food fight. Maybe that would make a better sports page picture.

It ended quickly enough, and I left the podium dripping with milk—tired, happy, and with a nice silver trophy and a $13,000 check for Novello Racing zipped into my pocket.

There was more celebrating back at the motor home. Sophie cooked everything she could find while Herb nursed and talked to the wounded Swift. Caroline replayed her video of the race for the rest of us, with play-by-play commentary from Rick in his best Daffy Duck voice. We ate, laughed, packed up, and then relaxed long into the evening in the warm glow of success.

Eventually exhaustion caught up with us. We all went back to the motel and slept in until mid-morning the next day. I had been fairly keen to return to the track for the Champ Car feature race, but that suggestion was met with a wall of blank stares from everyone. They loved racing our car, but watching somebody else didn't quite hold the same interest anymore. So, I went down to the pool to catch some sun. I pulled up a chair next to Allan and Herb.

"Well, Edward. A fine drive yesterday. What's next for you?" Allan asked.

I'd been avoiding thinking about that all weekend. What was next wasn't what I really wanted to do. I knew that yesterday's race had been a one-shot deal, but that taste of success in Formula Atlantic was going to make it very hard to go back to the Mustang.

"We'll return the Swift to Bill Baker, and then get busy on the Mustang, I guess. There's a Trans-Am race in three weeks in Portland, Oregon. And you?"

If we couldn't keep racing the Swift, I was at least secretly hoping that Allan Tanner might want to spend a little more time seeing more of the United States—specifically the Oregon coast with us. I was wrong.

"I'm booked on a flight back to England tomorrow," he said. "Herb's agreed to ship my gear over before you head back west. I've had several calls from a Formula Three team, and they want to talk to me in London right away. So I'll see what they have to say. Still, I must say that this has been fun. I have rarely eaten better, and I've greatly enjoyed the experience and the company. You have all done very well indeed. The ingredients are in place for a very strong team—especially the most important element."

"What's that?" I asked vacantly.

"I think that might be the driver. You, dummy," Herb offered helpfully.

Allan smiled and nodded in agreement.

"Quite right. I know that your friends are high on you as a driver, as friends always are. But to tell you the truth, Edward, I didn't expect much from your first race in an Atlantic car—and on an oval. Simply qualifying and finishing would have been enough. Rick designed an excellent wing, and the car was well prepared. But I must say that your performance yesterday was extraordinary.

"I've seen dozens of drivers come and go over the years. Only a few, a very few, have what I call the package. That's a natural feel for a racing car, a head for speed, and the ability to focus it. It's a rare gift, Edward; and for what it's worth, I believe that you have it. With a good car and the right people, you can go a long way in this sport."

I felt my face growing warm again. Unexpected compliments were embarrassing, especially coming from someone with the background and experience of Allan Tanner. While I appreciated his vote of confidence in my ability, what really stuck was his comment about "the right people." I knew that moving up to the higher levels of this sport demanded more than fast reflexes and a taste for speed. It also demanded a team effort: working with people whom I could literally trust with my life and learning from someone who knew how to get the most out of the car and a driver—someone as good as Allan Tanner. He had quickly forged us into a team that put a wrecked car and a rookie driver on the podium in its first race.

So it took that kind of team, and it also took serious money. Maybe if we had Raul DaSilva's wallet, we could have bought the Swift, hired Allan, and gone on to finish the Atlantic season. But none of us had that kind of money. In professional racing, dollars were always the essential ingredient. As much as I hated to admit it, I knew that we were one-race wonders. Much too soon, it was over.

Chapter 14

Reality

I wandered around the hotel for a while and then reluctantly went back to the room to pack. I found a note from Rick on my suitcase letting me know that he'd gone off to look at some electronics, and that there was some e-mail for me on his laptop from our website. I went to the desk, logged on, and retrieved two messages. The first was from my Dad, congratulating us on our run at Milwaukee, which he had watched and taped for me on ESPN.

The second e-mail was from a company named DynaSport Industries in New York City. It was marked Personal and Confidential. From the name, I assumed it was probably some sport drink outfit trying an Internet sales campaign. I was about to delete it as spam, but a sense of curiosity stopped me. Maybe I had been ignoring sport drinks all these years. I double-clicked on the file and read a one-page memo that nearly knocked me off the chair.

FROM:	*DynaSport Industries Inc.*
	J.R. Reynolds, President and CEO
TO:	*NovelloRacing.com*
	Attention: Eddie Stewart
	Personal and Confidential
SUBJECT:	*Sponsorship*

Dear Mr. Stewart,

I was in Milwaukee on business yesterday, and as a motorsport fan, I stayed on to take in the racing. The Formula Atlantic race was one of the best I've ever seen and you deserved to win it. I was very impressed with your performance, with the work of your team, and with what I've read on your website. From what I've read in the newspaper and on your site it appears that Milwaukee was your first and last race. That would be a shame.

I'll get straight to the point. I like sports, especially racing, and I like to back a winner. I think that you and your team deserve a chance to show what you can do for the rest of the season. I'm ready to talk to you about setting up some sponsorship to make that happen. Call me today.

J. R. Reynolds,
646-555-4859 ext. 233

I printed out the message and read it over three times. Then I checked the e-mail routing information to be sure it was genuine (you never knew with Rick). It was. I went to DynaSport's website, got a lot more information, and learned that in the last year, DynaSport Industries had gross sales in wholesale sporting goods of 246 million dollars in twenty countries worldwide. I then made two phone calls. The first call was to my Dad in Vancouver, who was a very sharp businessman and an accountant. He recognized both DynaSport and John Reynolds' names, and assured me that his company was the real thing. My second call was to the number on the e-mail, which was John Reynolds' personal cell phone. It rang once.

"John Reynolds."

"Mr. Reynolds, this is Eddie Stewart. I believe that you sent me an e-mail about sponsorship."

"Yes, I did, Eddie. Interested?"

"Yes, sir. Absolutely," I replied.

"Good. I meant what I said. I want to put something together to see you and your team through the rest of the season. When can you be in New York?"

New York? If I jumped in the truck and left now I might be there by tomorrow afternoon.

"How about 4:00 p.m. tomorrow?"

"No, it has to be early in the morning," Reynolds

replied firmly. "You be at the Milwaukee Airport Executive Jet gate at 6:00 a.m. My Gulfstream will have you here in an hour or so. OK?"

I swallowed hard. "OK."

"I look forward to meeting you," Reynolds said and hung up.

I stared at the phone in my hand. Then I realized what had just happened. This changed everything. In that brief conversation my stalled career as a Formula Atlantic driver had been restored and the team had a future. I went to the bathroom and splashed cold water on my face, dried off, and stared into the mirror.

"I am not dreaming," I said loudly to my reflection. I repeated it three times.

"Yes...you are," came a low, hollow voice from outside the bathroom. I spun around but saw no one.

The voice droned on. "This is your subconscious brain. I am tired of this dream. Go back to bed and wake up."

I crept forward and slowly poked my head around the corner...to find Rick kneeling beside the door, speaking into a plastic wastebasket.

Rick rolled onto his side in a fit of laughter. "Sorry, Eddie. But that was just too good to pass up."

"Yeah? Well, read this."

I went to the desk and handed him a copy of the DynaSport e-mail. Rick's smile quickly faded as he read it over twice and looked up at me in astonishment.

"Is this for real?" he asked.

"It is. I just got off the phone with Mr. John Reynolds. I'm meeting him in New York tomorrow morning to set up a sponsorship package. It's for real. He wants to see us finish the season!"

Rick sprang to his feet, grabbed my arm, flung the door open, and yelled, "Come on!"

We dashed down the stairs and ran outside. Allan and Herb were still relaxing in their deck chairs on the far side of the swimming pool. I slowed down to jog around to the other side. But Rick was in full flight; he raced straight ahead and into the pool, scattering little kids, plastic seahorses, and angry mothers. He thrashed his way through the water to the other side like a frenzied shark, and pulled himself out in front of Herb. I had already arrived and given Herb the e-mail copy to read.

Rick stood, dripping and breathless. "Herb... Allan... you've got to read it...we've got a sponsor...we can do it...the team...the season...," he sputtered.

Herb held up his hand for quiet as he read it. Then

he stood slowly, put one burly arm around Rick's shoulder and the other around me, threw his head back, and yelled, "YES!"

Then he pushed us both into the pool.

You just never know how things are going to go in this sport. We had started at the bottom of the ladder with a homebuilt car, hoping to get enough experience so we could move up to a professional formula racing series some day. "Some day" had arrived. Rescuing Bill Baker, confronting Raul DaSilva, and working hard had all come together to get us there in a hurry. Formula Atlantic had stopped being a dream. It was now a reality.

Two races remained in the series—Toronto and Miami. I was learn-
ing how to behave properly on the victory podium. With a powerful sponsor on board, I planned on getting some more experience on the podium very soon.

CART. Championship Auto Racing Teams.

Champ Car. A formula race car competing in the Champ Car World Series.

Downforce. The load placed on a car by airflow over its front and rear WINGS.

Formula Atlantic. A single-seat, open-wheeled race car.

Gearbox. Contains gears that the driver shifts to transmit engine power to the wheels.

Grid. The starting lineup of cars, which is based upon qualifying times.

Marshals. Racetrack safety workers.

Oversteer. When the rear wheels lose their grip and a race car slides or spins.

Pace lap. A slow warm-up lap before starting the race.

Pace car. The official car that leads the race car field during the pace lap or caution period.

Pit. The area where teams work on the race cars.

Pit board. A sign that is held up by the pit crew to inform their driver of place, race position, and lap.

Push. Another term for UNDERSTEER.

Podium. A stage where the top three race finishers receive their awards.

Pole position. The first starting position, which is awarded to the fastest qualifier.

Qualifying. Timed laps that determine where each car will be positioned at the start of the race.

Setup. Adjustments that are made to the race car by crew members.

Suspension. A system of springs, shocks, and levers that are attached to the wheels and support the race car.

Trans-Am. The Trans-American Championship for modified sports cars.

Understeer. When the front wheels lose their grip and the race car continues straight rather than turning.

Wings. Direct airflow that passes over the race car, pushing it down onto the track.

ANTHONY HAMPSHIRE is as comfortable strapped into the seat of a race car as he is in front of a classroom. Raised in London, England, and Calgary, Alberta, Anthony has been a racing driver and team manager, a football coach, and a magazine columnist. He was also a classroom teacher and educational technology consultant and is now a school principal. Anthony has earned national and provincial awards for his work in school curriculum and media, authored educational software, and is a regular conference presenter and workshop leader. He makes his home at the foot of the Rocky Mountains in Alberta, where he lives with his wife, two daughters, and a bossy Welsh Corgi.